The Edge of Redemption

A Novel

KATIE MORTON

WESTBOW·
PRESS
A DIVISION OF THOMAS NELSON
& ZONDERVAN

Author Credits: Edited by Elizabeth Ludwig.

Scripture taken from the Holy Bible, NEW INTERNATIONAL VERSION®.
Copyright © 1973, 1978, 1984 by Biblica, Inc. All rights reserved worldwide.
Used by permission. NEW INTERNATIONAL VERSION® and NIV® are
registered trademarks of Biblica, Inc. Use of either trademark for the offering
of goods or services requires the prior written consent of Biblica US, Inc.

WestBow Press books may be ordered through booksellers or by contacting:

WestBow Press
A Division of Thomas Nelson & Zondervan
1663 Liberty Drive
Bloomington, IN 47403
www.westbowpress.com
1 (866) 928-1240

Because of the dynamic nature of the Internet, any web addresses or
links contained in this book may have changed since publication and
may no longer be valid. The views expressed in this work are solely those
of the author and do not necessarily reflect the views of the publisher,
and the publisher hereby disclaims any responsibility for them.

Any people depicted in stock imagery provided by Thinkstock are
models, and such images are being used for illustrative purposes only.
Certain stock imagery © Thinkstock.

ISBN: 978-1-4908-4747-4 (sc)
ISBN: 978-1-4908-4748-1 (hc)
ISBN: 978-1-4908-4746-7 (e)

Library of Congress Control Number: 2014914579

Printed in the United States of America.

WestBow Press rev. date: 12/02/2014

For my dad,
who made the publication of this book possible

CHAPTER 1

Dark envelops me.

I shoot up, clutching my blankets to my chest. Sweat glues my nightdress to my body. My throat still aches, and my head still throbs from my present fever. Shrieks from outside my bedroom punch my ears. What is happening? My tongue dries inside my throat as my heart pounds against my chest. I whip off my covers, jump out of bed, then freeze. The ground beneath me trembles.

Moonlight slides through the window in the castle wall, throwing thin shadows over the room. I fumble to my bedroom door. A new noise bats my ears—the voice of one of my father's lords. I stop and listen, straining until my ears hurt.

"Awaken the princess! You there, open that door and awaken the princess!"

The door bursts open and almost slams into my head. Pants and gasps shake Lord Jonathan Wellington's body. His words trip over each other as he exclaims, "Thank goodness you're awake!"

"The noise woke me." I lift my chin and throw back my shoulders, hoping any anxiety doesn't show through. "Tell me what all this ruckus is about immediately."

A shadow flicks across his face. "Princess Lorelle ..." Though calm, his voice carries a deadly firmness. His eyes pierce me with a look that tells me he wants me to do something I know I will not want to do.

He adjusts the belt at his waist then draws his shoulders back. "Alandar has forced a surprise attack on us. This entire fortress, the palace and beyond, is under assault. Your precious life, my princess, is at risk. I am advising you and your mother to leave this kingdom at once and flee across the Jasmin Sea to Julinar where you will be safe until this deadly war is over."

I tilt my head. "Do you expect me to pack my things and board a ship for Julinar in the middle of the night?"

"That is exactly what I expect you to do."

His simple answer pricks me with firmness. I roll my fists together. No one tells me what to do. "Do you think, Lord Wellington, that I am not brave or capable enough to aid in this war?"

The heat in his gaze scorches me, but I don't care.

"It is not a matter of bravery or capability," he hisses. "It is a matter of your safety."

"Lorelle!" A scream sharper than a sword's blade echoes down the castle corridor.

My mother, her face drained and white, comes dashing out of the coal-black hallway toward us. Her eyes land on me. "Thank heaven you're all right. We must flee to a safer part of the castle."

Lord Wellington holds up his hand. "Your Majesty, you and Lorelle are boarding a ship for Julinar where you will be safe until this war is over."

The queen throws back her shoulders and pins the nobleman's gaze with hers. "I will not leave my country nor my people during this terrible time. Most of all, I will not leave King Norman. I will stay by my husband's side even if it costs me my life."

Reluctance sparks in Lord Wellington's eyes. "But, Your Majesty—"

"Silence!" My mother's tone could stop an entire army. "You have no authority over me." Her gaze then softens, and she lays a hand on Lord Wellington's arm. "I have to stay, Jonathan. A queen does not leave her people in time of trial."

Lord Wellington nods. "Very well, Your Majesty, but I must argue that this is no place for a seventeen-year-old." His gaze shifts to me.

My mother's eyes flicker for a moment, but then she nods, oblivious to my feelings about leaving the kingdom. "I completely agree."

Before I can even begin to argue, she rushes into my bedchamber and crosses to my storage closet. Flinging open the door, she reaches in and snatches a small carrier. "Lorelle," she exclaims, her anxiety raising her volume, "come over here and help me at once."

Reluctance pins me to the cold stone floor. Thirst scrapes at my throat, and my fever produces tiny beads of sweat on my forehead. My mother, however, continues packing in a haze of speed, and in a few minutes she has created a tall pile of clothes, personal belongings, and such in the carrier. After she squeezes it shut, she slams it to her chest. Just as she rushes over to me, a terrific force hits a castle wall near the bedchamber, causing us to collide and fall.

Lord Wellington leaps to our aid, his face darkening. "The West Entry! They're trying to knock down the entrance to the west wing!" Anxiety churns my stomach when I hear his next words. "The west wing was our escape route to Maniel Bay."

Agitation shakes my mother's voice. "Lord Wellington, you must—"

"The tunnel." His interruption falls out in a whisper.

"The tunnel?" A faint light seeps into the queen's eyes.

"The underground tunnel leading to the clearing next to Maniel Bay. We will be safe there, but we must be silent. There is a boat in the bay waiting to take Lorelle to a larger ship bound for Julinar."

My mother's cold fingers clasp mine. "Then let us make haste!"

As we slip through the doorway, another thunderous crash echoes through the castle and hurls us into a stone wall.

"If we don't get out of here fast, the ceiling may cave in on top of us." Lord Wellington's jaw tightens.

We pull ourselves to our feet and run through the dark. An icy sliver of moonlight, the only gleam of light in the room, chills the air around me. After a few minutes, Lord Wellington halts and drops to the floor. As my mother and I watch, he pries stones loose and pulls them out of the floor, one after another, until a wooden trapdoor appears. Grasping the rope handle on top, he pulls the door open, revealing a black ladder leading into complete darkness.

"Princess, down, quickly!"

Reluctance washing through me, I descend the icy iron ladder. Pain stitches over my knuckles from gripping the rods so tightly. When my foot lands on solid ground in place of a skinny ladder step, I almost collapse onto the dirt floor from surprise. A sea of black greets me – except the faint light slipping in from the trapdoor entrance, where Lord Wellington, following my mother, pulls the door shut. As the chill of the underground room seeps into the fabric of my dress, into my very bones, my shaking turns to shivering. Two warm arms wrap around me—my mother's— and I feel I will break in two.

A yellow glow flickers into the room, and through squinted eyes I see Lord Wellington striking a match for a second lantern. Now that light has smothered the darkness, I observe the room—dirt floor and walls stacked with antique weapons, chests, and armor. At the end of the room, a tunnel extends into pitch-blackness.

Lord Wellington hands my mother a lantern, and the three of us plunge into the gloom. Once swallowed inside, the cold air seems to slither into my body and freeze my blood. A third crash explodes above us, threatening to rip apart our ears. My tongue grates the roof of my mouth, rough as sandpaper.

Lord Wellington breaks into a run, and Mother and I have no choice but to follow. Light-headed and dizzy, my eyes strain and my feet drag with exhaustion. I try to keep my mind steady, but fever shakes my body.

After what seems like hours, we reach another iron ladder, and Lord Wellington ascends it and pushes the door at the top.

When it won't budge, doubt drenches me. I long to rush up to help, to do something—anything—but my sickness has enveloped me, stripping me of everything I have.

"Princess Lorelle, here." The lord's muffled voice trickles from above, slowly wending down to my ears. He hurries down the ladder and thrusts his lantern into my hands. Through a daze I see him climb back again and push with both hands and shoulders at the wooden door. It pops open. Relief flicks across his eyes as he grabs the ladder to maintain balance. Just beyond him I can barely make out grass, trees, and the endless night sky. He climbs out, and my mother gives me a push, nudging me upward. I think I hear shouts above me, but at the same time buzzing invades my ears. I'm not used to climbing with one hand. The flicker of the lantern I hold disappears as a breeze sweeps it away. I try to find the next bar to grasp onto, but I fail and slip. The lantern slides out of my hand and crashes to the floor.

My head spins again. What if I fall? The lantern's crash sounded thousands of feet below me. Seconds pass before I realize two strong hands hold my upper arms, and within a minute I lie on solid ground. My eyes dart in every direction. To my left Lord Wellington is talking to soldiers beside a small boat. Yet those strong hands are still holding me. I stand on my feet, supported by my rescuer. As I lift my head to his face, I see wind-blown blond hair and the brightest blue eyes I have ever seen.

I blink, and my mother stands in his place. The moonlight catches the tears brimming on her eyelids, and her hands tremble. She moves her fingers to my face and gently caresses my cheek. "My dear daughter, be brave, do not wither. Carry the dignity, boldness and strength as the daughter of the king of Aundria would do."

My eyes sting. I long to do more than stand still and powerless while my home and family are ripped from me. I want to wake up from the agonizing nightmare that grips me.

My mother reaches forward and touches her lips against my cheek. With one last caring look into my eyes, she says, "I love you."

The question of whether I will ever see her again weighs me down without mercy. I open my mouth to speak, but no words come. She must notice my struggle, for she gives me one last understanding smile.

Then she is gone. Before I could even tell her I loved her one last time.

Hands bigger than bricks lift me into a small lifeboat. I spin around to where I last saw my mother and catch sight of her and Lord Wellington descending back down the ladder into the tunnel.

My thoughts race to my father—where he is and if he is safe—and the same question concerning my mother now hits me a second time: Will I ever see either of my parents again?

I make out the noise of swishing water and then men's murmuring voices.

"She's about to faint, she is."

"We're almost to the ship."

"Do you think she can last that long?"

Do they speak of me or someone else? I struggle to keep my mind awake, but it keeps colliding with unbelief. I stare into the darkness, groping for something to hold on to, someone to depend on, but the thick of the night comes too close. Everything goes black.

CHAPTER 2

Sunlight streaks into my eyes. I wince and roll over into my pillow.

Then it hits me. Where on earth am I? Pain and hunger claw at my stomach, yet the burning ache and sweat of yesterday's fever have disappeared. I prop myself up on a wobbling elbow. The bed rocks beneath me. With a sweep of my eyes, I take in the compact, utterly wooden room. It holds nothing besides a small table next to my bed.

Disgusted at the contrast of the room to my own back home, I slip out of the bed and walk toward the single window, curiosity bubbling inside me like a fountain. When I gaze out, my jaw drops. Miles of water sparkle as far as I can see.

I am on a ship? I slump back to my bed and lean my head against the wall, searching for memories of the night before. An attack. Fleeing. Farewells. All flood back and crowd my mind.

I am on a ship bound for Julinar.

An icy wave of loneliness slams into me, with a backwash of homesickness. I squeeze my eyes shut, feeling as alone as the never-ending sea outside. My parents are back home, endless miles away, and I have no idea if they are safe or harmed. And my home, the grand Aundrian palace, does it still stand?

I blow out a twisted sigh. My eyes land on my small carrier at the foot of my bed. I snatch it up and rummage through it until I find my silver comb. As I brush out the tangles in my hair, I try to swallow down my uncertainty.

When my nerves finally quiet enough, I step to the door and grasp the handle. There is at least one fact that sends relief surging through me: that rotten fever has left my body. I open the small door and stop. A short hallway extends in front of me, with aging, wooden doors on each side. At the end of the hall stands a rickety staircase leading to a trapdoor at the top. Which way to go?

I straighten my shoulders and walk toward the steps. As I ascend, I can hear the shouts and cries of seamen above. After I reach the top, I slowly push open the door and climb out.

Men race in every direction, each one to his own duty. None turn their eyes my way, which leaves me to study my surroundings. The ship is fairly small but impressively decorated. The hand-carved rails, painted mastheads, and brass stanchions are the height of twelfth-century adornment. I feel relieved that the whole ship isn't as simple and dull as the little room downstairs.

"Princess Lorelle? Your Highness?"

I jump at the words. The speaker—a young man, tall and muscular, with wavy blond hair and incredibly blue eyes—stares back. I've seen that vibrant hue before, but where?

He straightens from a deep bow. "It is a relief to see you recovered."

Humiliation heats my cheeks as I remember my unconscious collapse the night before. "Thank you for your concern. I am perfectly well." I pull my shoulders straighter and reach my nose up, trying to make up for my lack of height compared to his.

"I'm glad to hear it." A warm smile lights his face. "I am Sir James Wellington." His shoulders lower in another bow.

Wellington? "I am honored to make your acquaintance, Sir Wellington." I extend my hand. As he kisses it, I ask, "Forgive me, but are you related to Lord Wellington?"

A hint of pride creeps onto his face. "I am. He is my father."

"Ah, your father," I repeat. "A fine man indeed. I owe my life to him." I instinctively breathe in as my heart jumps against my chest. "How was the battle when we left?"

His eyes dim. "Growing worse. We were lucky to escape. Thank goodness for that hidden waterway."

My stomach tenses. "And do you know anything concerning the safety of my parents?"

He runs a hand through his hair. "I am sorry, Your Highness, but I do not."

I swallow the urge to bite my lip. "Do you have any idea when we may know?"

"None. I'm afraid we have no choice but to wait."

The icy wave crashes into me again. "And how close are we to Julinar?"

His brow tightens. "Oh, I'd say a solid week before we arrive."

My throat tautens. A week? "Excuse me, but there appears to be some mistake concerning my room. The one I awoke in was small and simple. I was wondering if perhaps you could lead me to the cabin originally intended for me?"

His eyes spark, and I can't tell if it is laughter or critique. "I beg your pardon, Your Highness, but that *is* your permanent room. This ship is not lavish, and the rooms are quite simple. We have to make do with what we have." As I narrow my gaze and open my mouth to speak, he stops me with "At least yours has a window. Not many do."

"Sir Wellington, I do not believe you understood me correctly."

"Oh?"

His impertinence squeezes my patience to a pulp. "I am the crown princess of Aundria and am accustomed to a certain level of luxury. Obviously this ship is lacking, but I would have your finest and not the room downstairs."

"And perhaps you did not understand *me* correctly." His smile flashes with insolence. "That is your permanent room, my lady. The only ones finer are the quarters for the officers and the cabin for the captain."

I push my lips together as my gaze hardens. "Well, sir, if you refuse to help me, then I shall speak with the captain of this ship. Please direct me to him."

The glint in his eyes warns me not to meddle, but I ignore him. He points to a wooden doorway with a descending stairway. "His cabin is the last door on the right."

"Thank you." With a swish of my skirts, I turn and walk to the doorway. Once inside, I make my way down the hallway and knock on the last door.

"Come," a voice booms.

I turn the doorknob and step inside. A large room meets my gaze, one adorned with beautiful carvings, decorations, and furnishings. A man, his goatee and curled mustache the color of chestnuts, sits behind a desk bursting with rich, brown color. When his eyes land on me, he arises and bows. "Your Highness." His vibrant green eyes sparkle. "It is an honor to be in your presence."

With long strides, he crosses to me as I extend my hand. He grasps my fingers and presses his lips upon them. "I am Lord Andrew Harmon."

Pleased with his manners, I curtsy as his lips leave my hand, which is such a contrast to his strong fingers. "I am honored to make your acquaintance, Lord Harmon."

A smile appears beneath the mustache. "You seem to have recovered quickly."

"Fortunately, yes." I flash my prettiest smile. His manner comforts me, warming me like a thick blanket.

"I hope our humble ship meets well with you."

I sweetly fold my hands and step forward. "Oh, it is a beautiful ship, but there seems to be some mistake concerning my room. The one I am in now is inadequate. Perhaps you could lead me to the chamber originally intended for me?"

His brow wrinkles, and he adjusts the belt at his waist. "Ah, Your Highness, I beg your pardon, but we do not have many grand rooms on this ship. The only one that is a bit more formal is this one. If you wish, you may spend most of your afternoons here. I am usually preoccupied with other matters during that time, so you will be undisturbed."

Chagrin kicks me in the ribs, but I rally and regain my wits. "Thank you, Lord Harmon. Your kindness is appreciated."

A hint of sorrow flashes in his eyes. "I know that you were forced to leave your family and home last night. This ship is probably an extreme contrast to what you are used to, but I promise I will do everything in my power to make it a comfortable and easy voyage for you. We will arrive in Julinar in about one week. Once there, you will be made at home in my estate. I assure you, you will be satisfied with the lodgings. In the meantime, if there is anything I can do for you, please do not hesitate to let me know."

I like this man. His kindness and strength remind me of my father. I know if the need should arise, I can wholly depend upon his service and protection.

My lips spread in a smile. "Again, I thank you."

He bows, and after a curtsy of my own, I exit the room. My, what a contrast he is to that roguish young man I met on deck! As I stride up the stairs, the sparkle of the water catches my eye. I stroll to the railing and rest my hands on the smooth surface, shoving away any thoughts of home. Wave after wave rolls onto the side of the ship until it all becomes a blur in my eyes. Lately, everything has been so sudden; I feel as if I'm not really living what is happening now.

My thoughts drift to King Maurice. Hate seethes in my gut. I grip the wood until white washes over my knuckles. The grief he has sliced open still stings me. I know it will never leave. He has burned it into me.

Why has he cursed his people with such cruelty? What feeds such a burning hate for my father? Yet I know. My father aided the suffering Alandarins and established a home for the runaways in Julinar.

Julinar. Such a beautiful island. I will be there in one week, beholding its famous beauty and plentitude for myself. Tarnishing that loveliness is the dirt that started a war.

As I watch the waves, the face of a young girl appears in the water. Laughing and joyful, her blue eyes sparkle, and her smile shines. Her cheeks are as red as apples, and tiny dimples crease her face.

I blink. The water returns to calm, quiet waves. My eyes smart as the hatred in my stomach thickens.

Always happy, always together. No one could stand between us. Our whole lives had been attached to the other. Until that one night—that one dark night that left me shivering with cold and fear.

"A ship!"

I jerk up my head.

A young sailor, posted high above the deck, strains over the railing, his gaze locked on the horizon. I follow his gaze and spot for myself a tiny black dot miles away.

The sailor lifts a spyglass to his eyes and shouts, "It's Alandarin. There's an Alandarin flag!"

Gasps whoosh from sailor to sailor. Many rush to the railing beside me, all eyes searching.

"Do they know we have the princess?" someone yells.

I twist my fingers. I know why they would want me, but what would they do with me once they had me?

I breathe in and whisk the train of worry away like a fly. I have absolutely nothing to fear. The captain will let nothing whatsoever happen to me.

Hands lock on me and hurl me into a corner. Shocked, I raise a curled fist when my eyes meet those of my attacker. Blue—intense and commanding.

I stiffen and try to jerk away. "What do you think you're doing? How dare you!"

The young man flattens his lips and remains silent. My gaze slides over his shoulder. Lord Harmon calls out as he passes by, "Good work, Wellington. Keep her there for a minute."

I turn back to Sir Wellington and dig my eyes into his. "I demand to know what on earth is going on. You have absolutely no right to—"

His smirk cuts me off. "You never hesitate to jump to conclusions, do you? I'm not trying to hurt you. You were completely visible over there, staring out over the deck." He swings an arm toward the railing. "The other ship could have easily spotted you with just one spyglass."

"Fine," I retort. "But next time, why not use words? I do have ears, you know."

A shorter man taps Sir Wellington on the shoulder. "I'll see to her, sir."

Sir Wellington pivots and stalks off without so much as a by your leave. The other sailor, his body reminding me of a squashed pig, escorts me downstairs and out of sight, to Lord Harmon's cabin.

After he leaves me, I sink into a chair, discouragement and homesickness pressing in on me.

It can only be so long. It can only be so long that I will have to sit and wait at Lord Harmon's estate until this abhorrent war has run its course.

My throat tightens. The ship rises over a swell, and a wave slams into the cabin's window.

CHAPTER 3

My stomach churns. I groan, curl into a ball, and roll over on my bed for the one-millionth time. When the ship cants to the right, I practically slide off. I know it is just a matter of time before the contents of my stomach will rise to my mouth.

Flipping to my back, I stare out the single porthole. Rain slaps the glass, never slowing. Lightning streaks into the room every few seconds, and the following thunder nearly deafens me. One more minute cooped up in this miserable little room and I will scream.

I drag myself off the bed, my head swirling, and stumble to the door. Navigating the corridor, I feel like a baby being flung about in a cradle by a demented nanny. The movement twists my stomach. A sour taste rises to my throat. I panic, trying to swallow it down, but it only rises higher. I need to get to some open area—and quick.

Slapping a hand over my mouth, I race down the hall, ramming into walls, and streak up the stairs and through the trapdoor. But I'm not at all prepared for the surprise that awaits me.

Rain needles my face. The wind practically knocks me flat, and waves wash over the gunwale. Men race in every direction, all shouting. If I survive this storm, I will be living a miracle.

Reminded of my predicament by a swirling in my belly, I dash to the railing and lean over the side. What little I've eaten doesn't take long to empty, and I slide into a heap on the deck. I need to get back downstairs, but along with every ounce of food in my body, all my energy has been spewed out on the waves.

As I sit there, huddled and shivering, an icy wave thrashes over the side of the ship, drenching me to the bone. For a few seconds I can hardly breathe. Shakes ripple through my body, and my vision blurs.

"Whoa! Hold on 'ere!"

A tall, thin sailor rushes toward me, his hand outstretched.

"Yeer Highness! What on earth are ye doing here?" He drops down to his knees next to me.

I push up on wobbly legs and nearly collapse into the sailor's arms.

"Ah, I see," he practically shouts into my ear. "Yee've been tasting a bit of the nasty sea. C'mon, let me get ye out o' here."

He slings an arm around my shoulder, and as I walk next to him—or more like drag next to him—I wonder how on earth he can be so calm in the midst of such a storm. My gaze darts across the deck, and I spot that young, blue-eyed officer, shouting orders a few yards away. When our eyes meet, he rushes over.

Cupping his hand to his mouth, he shouts above the howl of the wind, "What's going on?"

"Sick! She's sick!" the sailor hollers back.

A thin smile spreads across the young man's face. "Really? Again?"

Anger chokes me as much as my earlier sickness.

"Aye, sir." The sailor nods. "Where shall I put her?"

"Stay on deck," Sir Wellington orders. "I'm heading to Captain Harmon's cabin anyway. I'll take her along with me."

"Well and good!" With a dip of his head, the sailor releases my elbow, and I wobble.

"Easy, now." Sir Wellington sweeps me into his arms, settling me against his solid chest. "Let's get you away from this railing."

Was that compassion or mockery in his voice? Either way, I simply nod. I'm more than ready to get away from that railing.

"I'm sure this gale caught you off guard."

"A gale?" I lift my face to be heard as the wind almost snatches away my words. "This is only a gale?"

"What did you think it was?"

I just remain silent.

When we reach Lord Harmon's door, Sir Wellington bangs against it with his foot. "Captain Harmon!"

The door swings open to a startled Lord Harmon. "Good Lord! What's happened?" His eyes hit me. "Come in."

The warmth and security of the cabin surrounds me as Sir Wellington lays me down on a plush sofa in a corner of the chamber. My once-churning stomach now turns into a brick.

"She just got a little nauseous." He looks down at his hand on my shoulder and draws it away. "But she'll be all right."

I roll over, still dizzy, and stare out the dark window, wishing to disappear.

"Very well. While Her Highness rests, let us rechart our course. I fear this wind has altered our bearings."

Lord Harmon's deep voice drones on. And on. Eventually, it lowers to a buzz in my ears while I mull over why a lord—head of Julinar's capitol and a ship's captain—would converse with such a churlish man as Sir Wellington. Sir Wellington is only a knight—hardly anything to compare with a lord.

Barely had that last thought flitted through my head before the room around me melts into a blur.

Banging slams into my dream of home, a home with two safe parents that is undisturbed by a war. The banging is followed by a low, muffled voice. "Captain Harmon?"

I jerk awake and sit up, snapping my head toward the door. It rattles in the frame with the next round of knocking.

"Captain Harmon, sir?" the voice demands again.

Why would someone pound on my door requesting the captain? My gaze slides from the door, to the brass wall sconces, and settles upon the red sofa where I rest. Of course. I fell asleep in the captain's quarters.

My tongue rises to the roof of my mouth as I swallow. Have the captain and Sir Wellington gone up to the deck? How long have I been here?

The knock sounds again. My eyes lock on the door. It would not suit to be found here unchaperoned.

I hold my breath, waiting for the caller to give up and go away. Eventually the noise ceases, and I rise—then stop. Something is different. I spin and look toward the window. Sunlight stabs my eyes. Apparently, the storm has passed.

Relief washes over me, energizing me. I walk out of the cabin and up the stairs. Golden light bathes the ship's masts and shimmers off the sails. Thank goodness. The vigorous activity I'd witnessed earlier on deck has calmed to a much smoother level.

The pool of sparkles beckons me to the railing. As I walk over, the ship crests a wave and plunges back down. My feet shift on the deck as someone rams into me.

"Whoa! I beg your pardon, Your Highness."

I groan inside as Sir Wellington bends in a bow. Why is this man somehow always behind me?

He smiles. "I am glad to see you're up and well."

The last thing I want to do is repeat the conversation we had on my first day on the ship, five days ago.

I level my gaze at him, not moving. "I am. If you'll excuse me ..."

I push past him and continue to the ship's side. An older sailor, sweaty and unshaved, makes his way over to me as he cleans the railing. The dense odor of sweat and fish surrounds him. He seems to not notice me, instead busying himself with his cleaning. I am disgusted at his appearance, but curiosity concerning Sir Wellington pushes me forward.

I ease up next to him. "Excuse me, sir."

He spins and locks eyes with me. "Wah?" a thick voice crawls through his lips.

17

I try not to stare at the red streaks netting over his eyeballs. "That ship that was spotted a few days ago. Has it been sighted since?"

He runs a gnarly hand through hair that resembles a rat's nest. "Nay, ma'am … er … Your Highness. 'Tis gone fer sure."

"I see." I tap my fingers on the railing, debating how reliable a source this man really is. "And Sir Wellington … do you know his position on this ship?"

"Aye, he's the captain's first mate." He bypasses me and swipes his rag along the brass rail.

First mate? Surprise broadsides me. I knew he was a knight but certainly did not consider first mate. How did he come to claim that position?

Facing me again and still scrubbing away at the railing, the sailor continues, "Since we had to leave so abrupt the night of the attack, the crew was put together quick. I heerd that the king chose his most trusted men to protect his daughter." He glances over his shoulder, a knowing smile revealing rotted, twisted teeth. A muffled snort follows.

I have only just finished drinking in the information when coughs shake through him. He hurls a chunk of something out of his mouth and over the side.

I stare at him, horror steaming in my belly. Need to get away from the repulsive man shivers through me. "I thank you, sir." I tip my head and quickly leave him.

I rush over to the other railing, still shuddering from the show I was just given. Once I reach my destination, I relax and, in short order, again become covered with the awe of the sea's beauty.

My skin prickles as the realization of someone standing next to me sweeps through the air. I turn my gaze. "Sir Wellington." I stiffen. "Is there something you need?"

"No, Your Highness. I simply came to admire the view." The blue water enhances his vibrant eyes. "It is amazing, isn't it?"

His words confuse me. The flutter in my chest increases. "So …" I draw in a deep breath and lift my chin. "I understand you are Lord Harmon's first mate. Is that true?"

A ghost of a smile lights his face, and he turns and settles his gaze on me. "That is correct."

"How is it that you came to claim that position?"

Sir Wellington's eyes shift back to the water. "On the night of the attack, your father quickly chose Lord Harmon and me as the head commanders of this ship." He turns to me, his blue eyes twinkling. "He wanted to make sure his daughter was safe."

I avert my gaze, cheeks burning like hot coals. I hate being watched out for like a young child, especially by someone as arrogant as Sir James Wellington. "So you consider yourself worthy of that distinction then?"

"I take no credit for myself. I am honored King Norman chose me for the role. He has done so much for our country in his life; it is the least I can do to serve him in any way I can."

I cock my head. Beneath his usual sarcasm and teasing, something deeper dwells—humility. Loyalty.

Heart picking up speed, I dare a peek at his face, but he's returned to gazing out to sea. I follow his lead, staring into the blue myself, a sudden urge to know more about this young man welling inside me.

"Since your father is a lord, I assume your mother is a lady?"

When no answer comes, I cast him a sideways glance. A dark, cold sheet covers his face. His eyes flash with sorrow, and I instantly regret the question.

He turns to me, solemn lines etched on each side of his mouth. "Yes, Your Highness. My mother was a noble. She died of disease when I was seven."

I suck in a breath. Pain needles my stomach as a memory stirs. Grief is all too familiar to me.

My thoughts race to my own mother—back home in Aundria. It was hard enough bidding her farewell, so the thought of losing her almost chokes me.

This man—strong and noble—now seems nothing more than a young boy, lonely and forgotten, longing for a loved one.

"I am sorry," I whisper. "Please accept my condolences."

A faint smile softens his face. "Thank you."

"Sir Wellington!" A tall, lean sailor strides over to us, his eyes fixed on Sir Wellington. "Lord Harmon ordered me to inform you that we made better time than he expected. We will arrive in Julinar tomorrow."

CHAPTER 4

A gull cries and flaps onto the top of the mast. I lean over the railing, trying to drink in everything my eyes can see of Julinar. Lush and green, the island glimmers with tall, proud trees, rivers that sparkle like strings of diamonds, and mountains that seem to touch the tip of heaven. I can barely make out the beginning of the village of Camwind, so well does it blend in with the surrounding beauty. Never has a place looked so inviting, for the idea of getting off this claustrophobic ship sounds like a sweet melody. Julinar, I am sure, will be a perfectly fine place for me to live for the time being.

Ever since we spotted land a few hours ago, anticipation has bubbled up inside of me like a fountain. To step foot on solid land, to witness actual civility and to inhabit a genuine building ...

Oh, I could never survive being a sailor.

Sir Wellington's voice booms, "Make ready for port!"

As sailors rush to fulfill their duties, a crowd begins forming near the harbor, curious about the unexpted ship. When they spot me, surprise flies onto their faces. Then the cheering erupts. Amid the shouts, people push and struggle past each other as they clammer to make it to the front of the crowd. The noise mounts as the ship inches closer. I run my hands over the gunwale and watch as more people rush from the village and out to the port, joining the croud in shouting and waving once they see me.

Turning my attention to the activity on the ship, I realize I'm not the only important cargo aboard. Apparently, valuable Aundrian goods were rushed onto the ship as well. Sailors roll crates onto the dock and into the street. No one on the ship seems to notice me, though the people of Julinar cry out my name without stop.

Thinking I have been forgotten, I march to the gangplank and try to squeeze through the press of sailors. A tug on my arm yanks me from my exit. Just as suddenly, the grip releases, and I stumble into scrambling sailors. In their rush, I ram into the railing, just about flipping over. Hands grasp my shoulders to stop my fall, but after they release I once more stagger backward. Enough is enough!

Suspecting the likely culprit, I whirl and say, "Do you have a problem with personal space, Sir Wellington?"

His gaze holds mine. "You're not allowed to exit the ship yet, Your Highness." His voice carried a cool tone, but I detect annoyance swimming in its depths.

"Exit the ship?" Anger heats my cheeks. "And why ever not, may I ask?"

That teasing, laughing look leaps into his eyes. "Because"—a smile tugs his lips—"your father specifically instructed me to keep a close watch on you and escort you wherever you go once we reach Julinar."

My immediate embarrassment and annoyance rushes up my neck like spreading fire. My fingers itch with desire to slap the grinning face before me, but I keep them firmly clenched at my sides. "Oh he did, did he?"

If only tones could kill. Sir Wellington merely narrows his eyes, which only angers me further. "Thank you, Sir Wellington, but I would frankly rather walk alone."

With that I spin and hurry off. As I make my way to the gangplank, a short sailor stops me. "Excuse me, Your Highness." His words squeak, matching the rest of his chubby body. He holds up my brown carrier. "I believe this is yours."

"It is, thank you." I snatch the carrier's handle and pull it from him.

He wilts into a bow. "Your Highness."

"Yes, Your Highness," Sir Wellington breaks in. "You may come with me."

Irritation curls my fingers into fists. The compassion I felt for him yesterday concerning his mother now makes me want to laugh at myself.

From the corner of my eye, I notice his extended arm, but I am anything but willing to take it.

Averting my gaze, I thrust my carrier into his chest and sweep down the gangplank, skirts swishing and shoulders rolled back. Many of the people in the streets bow when my feet hit the ground—but not all.

A number of rough, drunk men swarm over me, crying, "Your Highness! Oh, Your Highness! We're so glad ye have come!" Some kneel to kiss my feet; others try to embrace me.

Liquor reeks from their mouths. I scramble to get free, but their clasps lock tighter. The heat from their bodies moves in with suffocating force.

Alarm is just beginning to take hold when two firm hands tear me from the men.

"I think your father had a point." Sir Wellington's firm voice cuts through the rabble.

When he offers his arm the next time, I accept it.

———◄o►———

A pebble wiggles into my shoe as I crunch over the gravel, eyeing the mansion of Lord Harmon's estate. Though not a castle, the mansion is impressive, claiming a large chunk of the island to house its massive size. Towers climb from the sides and roofs. Lord Harmon, Sir Wellington, and a few soldiers accompany me up the marble steps and through the giant pillars to the doorway settled between ivy-covered walls. Two huge oakwood doors stand open, welcoming us. Inside, sunlight streams through windows that cover almost entire walls. Stairways twirl upward, where I see countless more hallways and rooms. Satin and silk drape from the ceilings, and gold sconces and mounted armor glint from the walls below.

As I stand there, drinking it all in, Lord Harmon's voice breaks into my thoughts.

"Thank you, Sir Wellington. You may leave the princess to me, now."

After handing Lord Harmon my carrier, the young knight bows and strides away. Relief loosens the muscles in my shoulders, yet a tiny tinge of regret prickles my spine. When Lord Harmon extends his arm, I smile away my thoughts and walk beside him along a tapestry-lined hallway.

"I will now have you meet Lord Ashton Barkinten, overseer of this estate while I am gone."

Like deep music, his words echo from the ceiling high overhead. When we reach one of the hallway's offices, the lord and I enter the room where a young man, tall and striking, sits behind a desk. Immediately he arises.

"Lord Harmon!" He lowers himself in a bow. "How good it is to see you."

"And you, Lord Barkinten. Allow me to introduce Princess Lorelle, daughter of King Norman and Queen Isabel of Aundria."

The young man bows again, his head down. "Your Highness." At my signal of approval he rises, a grin lighting his face. "I am truly honored."

I smile as he turns to a servant standing in a corner. "Summon my wife, please."

After the servant disappears out the door, Lord Barkinten returns his gaze to me. "I hope you had an easy and pleasant voyage." His brown eyes appear carefree, but I notice them spark with concern. Obviously he wonders why I have arrived so unexpectedly.

"Yes, thank you."

"Indeed," Lord Harmon says. "We made better time than I anticipated."

I study the room. Gold, silk, and jeweled adornments catch my eye everywhere I looked. Julinar, itself overflowing with beauty, doesn't hesitate to bathe its buildings in glamor either.

The servant appears at the door again with a young woman in tow. Hair cascades like a gold waterfall down her shoulders, while her blue eyes sparkle like sapphires. When her lips spread into a smile, I can't stop my own from following.

"Your Highness, allow me to introduce my wife, Lady Angelet." Lord Barkinten offers his hand to her as she approaches. "My dear, this is Her Highness, Princess Lorelle of Aundria."

The woman lowers in a graceful curtsy. "Your Highness, I am honored."

The presence of another female sends excitement flowing through me. Thrill that I will be living where she lives swims after it.

The lord waves his hand to the servant. "You may take Lady Angelet and Princess Lorelle to Her Highness's room."

After Lord Harmon hands off my carrier, the servant leads us up a grand flight of stairs. As we follow him, Lady Angelet turns her head to me. "What has brought you to our humble abode, Your Highness?"

I hesitate, the thought of my fleeing dimming the pleasure I've felt since arriving. "King Maurice led a surprise attack on Aundria's fortress." Hatred boils in my stomach. "I was forced to flee for my life."

A pause hugs the air.

"I see." The words fall out gently, but my ears sense the shock that pushes them forward. "I am so sorry. Truly, I am." Her eyes brim with sympathy. "Have you any idea if our fortress still stands?"

"None," I reply, curling my skirts in my hands as we climb the steps. That same question has weighed me down the entire week. How I long to hear some news!

"Your Highness, I promise we will do everything in our power to create a comfortable and warm atmosphere here for you.

Leaving your home and family so abruptly must have been far from easy. Please accept my condolences."

My heart flutters. Lady Angelet's mannerisms pull back memories of my mother. I finger a curl on my neck.

When we enter a hallway filled with sconces and draped cloths, the servant stops, opens one of the doors, and bows. "Your Highness."

I step inside. Blue silk curtains, lined with gold thread, grace a window. A bed stands against the center wall, with a large headboard designed with gold carvings and scattered jewels. A satin cloth, its color reminding me of my days by the railing, hangs from the top.

I walk to a wardrobe standing planted against one wall, where I run my hand over the smooth wood tinted with red and curl my fingers around the thick gold handle. My reflection catches my eye in a mirror that stands above a vanity table next to a lounge chair. I look above it to the walls. A sky-blue shade arrests them, while a gold cloth, fringed with dangling frills, drapes from corner to corner.

Seeing such a room makes me never want to step foot on a ship again, until my return home, at least. I sigh and let my delight stretch a smile across my face.

"Does this suit you?" Lady Angelet folds her hands together in front of her.

My eyes sweep the room. "Yes, thank you. This will do just fine."

After the lady leaves the room, I sit on the bed and stare at the wall. All of this is beautiful, but it isn't my real home. What is my home like now? An icy wave of uncertainty washes over me. Alandar started by attacking Aundria. What if they defeated Aundria and proceeded to Julinar next?

Chapter 5

Aknock echoes in my bedchamber.

A sigh slips from my lips. "Come."

The door opens, and a servant creeps inside. After a bow, he lifts an arm toward the door. "Your Highness, Sir James Wellington."

The blue-eyed knight enters and bows. "Your Highness, I have come to inform you that an Aundrian ship has been spotted."

I jump up, surprise and excitement tingling in my fingertips. "Thank you, Sir Wellington. How far away is it?"

"I would guess by its distance that it will enter the harbor in about two hours."

Two hours! Oh, how I have longed for the moment when I would receive news, and now, it stands only two hours away. Yet why did the knight come to tell me himself, instead of sending a servant?

"If you wish," he continues, "I can escort you to the harbor when it arrives."

Ah, that was it. I pause, reluctant to accept. However, his eyes don't hold his usual all-knowing look, and my mind wanders back to my first day in Julinar and my first encounter with Julinarin sailors. Finally I give in.

"Thank you, Sir Wellington. I greatly appreciate your offer. I will accept."

A warm smile lights up his face, and after a bow, he leaves the room.

I will never be able to figure that man out. His sarcasm drives me nearly mad, but his unwavering strength and dignity pique my interest. He always seems to have a secret—something that keeps him joyful and confident. I'm determined to discover what he knows.

I move to my vanity and sit, gazing into the mirror at the girl who stares back. I smile as I pick out her attractive features. My parents have always called me beautiful. For the first time, I try to see myself objectively—sparkling brown eyes, eyelashes that curl to perfection, and a smooth complexion, thanks to my nursemaid's many ministrations. My chestnut-brown hair ripples behind my ears, thick but soft. I have already been eyed by many men of noble rank, but most have pursued me because of my title. One of my maids once mentioned marrying her husband for financial support. I shiver. The thought of an arranged marriage, of not marrying for love, turns my blood cold.

Two hours later another knock sounds on the door. I smooth down my hair and beckon Sir Wellington to enter. Rising, I accept his extended arm, and we leave the room.

As we make our way to the estate's door, Lord Harmon, Duke Barkinten, and Lady Angelet join us. I am relieved I won't have to be alone with Sir Wellington, and my tight shoulders relax.

The noise and excitement of the streets fill the air as we walk outside. Many of the citizens bow and make a straight path for us, while the harbor itself seems to call me. When we finally come upon it, the ship slides into the dock.

The sight of my country's flag rouses memories of home and family. Worry shivers under my skin like the sharp breeze around me. Are they all right?

After the ship drops anchor, a man, his height reaching for the clouds, sets foot on the dock. I recognize him as one of my father's noblemen, Lord Richard Williams. His eyes scan the crowd, and when they land on me, relief leaps into them. He quickens his pace and strides the length of the dock toward me.

"Your Highness!" He bows at the waist. "I am relieved to find you here safe and secure."

I smile. "Yes, thank you. It is a pleasure to see you again, Lord Williams."

He smiles as well, but his gaze sparks with anguish. My heartbeat picks up speed.

Another lord and a number of knights ascend the platform in the middle of the village and hush the crowd. Anxiety roots my feet. I turn from Lord Williams and steal glances at the four faces beside me. The traces of worry on them are obvious.

"Your Highness, I need to speak with you immediately and privately."

My stomach sours. "Certainly."

"Duties here do not yet allow me to travel to the mansion with you, but is it acceptable if we talk in the cabin of my ship?"

I nod. "Of course."

He looks over my head to the four behind me. "If you will accompany us, I would be very grateful."

My fingers stick to my palms with sweat. Lord Williams offers his arm, and the six of us ascend the gangplank and make our way to his cabin. It is smaller than Lord Harmon's cabin and lacking in adornments and furniture. Simple wooden chairs line the walls, but no one bothers to sit.

Lord Williams fumbles for a moment. A deadly silence punches the air, sending chills down my spine. He adjusts his waistcoat. "Your Highness, tragedy has struck us. As you know, your mother and Lord Jonathan Wellington were retreating to safety in the underground tunnel. Soldiers, ordered by King Maurice"—he swallows—"found them and killed them on the spot."

My heart stops. My breathing stops. Everything blurs. Gasps all around pierce my ears. A lump thicker than anything I have ever experienced chokes me. I gulp, clench my fists, and force myself to look at Lord Harmon. The shock in his eyes only chills my blood more, so I look away. My eyes land on Sir Wellington.

The young knight's gaze is fixed on a chair, his arms folded at his chest, with one hand holding his chin. His jaw and shoulders are locked. Only his blue eyes show the agony consuming him.

"I am so sorry, Your Highness." Lord Williams' words fill the empty silence.

I need to get out of here. I need to be alone. Now.

"Lord Harmon." My voice is barely above a whisper. "Please escort me back to the estate."

He tips his head, brow furrowed. I clasp his offered arm and grit my teeth, desperate to keep from crying. As we leave the ship, tears smart my eyes. I blink them back, praying they won't spill down my cheeks.

After what seems like hours, the mansion comes into view. We walk through the doors, my swallowed sobs making my chest heave. Once inside, I break loose from Lord Harmon's grasp. I force my lips apart and say, "Thank you, Lord Harmon and Lady Angelet."

Then, before the sobs can rush through my lips, I turn and flee up the staircase. My feet race faster than my mind can think. Now that I am finally out of sight of people, I let the tears stream down my cheeks, their warmth heating my face. When I reach my bedchamber, I fling the door open and run inside. I shove my back against it, slamming it shut.

Then I sink into a heap.

---〈o〉---

"Princess Lorelle?" A gentle voice—a woman's—breaks my heavy silence, followed by a soft tapping on my bedroom door. "Please allow me to enter."

I lift my head from my bed, where I have been lying for the past few hours, and shift my eyes from the wall to the window in front of me. The sun is melting into the horizon, disappearing beneath the waves. I lift my hand and pull straggly hair from my face to behind my ears.

"Princess Lorelle? Please let me in."

I roll from my side to my stomach, eyelids heavy and head throbbing.

The doorknob scrapes behind me, but my gaze remains fixed on the wall, blurred with tears. Footsteps cross the room to my bed, and someone eases onto the mattress beside me. A hand rests on my shoulder.

"Oh, my dear ..." Lady Angelet's voice breaks as she strokes my tangled hair. "Are you all right?"

I let my head tumble down between my arms, my face buried in the bed. The pain of grief digs into me more sharply than it did when I first met it years ago. I lost one person then. Now my mother makes it two.

"I am so sorry," Lady Angelet says.

There is a pause, and the stillness buzzes in my ears.

Her fingers gently make their way through my hair to my neck. "You have every right to be sorrowful. Nothing can ease the pain of losing a mother. Nothing I can say will lessen your hurting, but I do know how your mother was so very proud of you. You were a loyal, loving daughter, Your Highness, and she loved you as much as a mother can love her daughter, if not more. She was a strong and courageous and loving queen."

Silence fills the air, and I bite down on my lip, my eyes on the white pillow to my side.

"I want you to know that I'm here for you. If there's anything you need, don't be afraid to talk to me. This is a hard burden to carry, I know, and I don't want you to shoulder it alone. I offer you all the support and encouragement I can." She brushes the hair away from my eyes. "Are you all right?"

"No," I manage to squeak out. After a pause, I finally gather the courage to turn my head and look her in the eye. "Why did this happen?"

She sighs heavily. "I don't know. We don't always have the answers to tragedies such as these."

Unconsciously, I shift my head to her lap. She wipes the tears from beneath my eyes and then brushes her fingers over my forehead. "Oh, Lorelle."

31

My ears perk. Only my mother and father call me Lorelle. No one else has been allowed to call me anything but Your Highness or Princess Lorelle. But here, right now, it's comforting and feels exactly right.

My hand searches for hers, and when I find it, I clasp it, almost hurting my fingers I hold so tightly. She squeezes back. "I do know, though, that God longs for you to accept His endless supply of love, peace, strength, joy, and comfort." She leans forward and kisses my head. "Think on that for a while."

Chapter 6

I pull back the bowstring and release, sending my arrow whizzing through the air. It strikes one circle away from the bull's-eye. I reach down, grab another arrow from my quiver, and send it flying. Satisfaction sweeps over me as it hits dead center.

I lower my bow as my waiting servant clears the target, and I let my gaze wander to the forest surrounding the small archery field. Fresh air fills my lungs as I breathe in deeply. The light from the sun warms my face and neck, and the leaves rustle gently in the treetops. I should have been out here sooner. I spent the day yesterday, the day after I was delivered the news by Lord Williams, alone in my room, processing and trying to recover from the stab. Only this afternoon have I ventured out.

A bird flies over my head and disappears into the leaves of a tree. The tension in my chest tightens as my thoughts wrap around my father. Lady Angelet, after being informed by Lord Williams, told me my father had withdrawn into privacy for a few days to grieve. His lords were continuing on with his affairs, but duty dictated that his grieving time would be cut short. Knowing he is mourning the loss of his wife and carrying the weight of a war on his shoulders, alone, cuts across my heart like a freshly sharpened knife.

I swallow and shoot another arrow. The arrow hits the exact spot where my previous arrow struck: perfectly in the center.

"I had no idea you were such a skilled archer."

I tense, recognizing the voice of Sir James Wellington. I keep my back turned. "Yes. My father is quite accomplished at the sport, and he taught me well."

As I grasp another arrow and position it, I hear him come closer. Ignoring him, I pull back the bowstring and release.

"May I be so bold as to ask how are you doing?" His voice being low and grave, I know it is more than just a question of politeness.

"I'm all right." I try to keep my focus on my archery, severely hoping my mind won't settle on my mother. I busy myself watching the servant clear the target for me.

His silence indicates he does not believe me. "Honestly?"

My heart twists. I try to stop the thought, but within an instant, out of my control, it comes.

I roll my chin as I swallow, but the lump in my throat only rises higher. Tears are swelling, swelling ... but I will absolutely not let this young man see my true emotions.

I throw back my head and turn toward the knight. His blue eyes level with mine. "Sir Wellington, I am as all right as one can be after the loss of a dearly loved one."

He studies me. Already he seems to know how I truly feel. "If there was anything I could do for you ..."

I turn and clasp another arrow, eyeing the flat, green field. With a few steady movements, I send it streaking through the air. "King Maurice is a selfish and brutal man. The pain he has caused my family will never leave." I pause. "You have no idea what he has done to us." My hands run over the wood of the bow. "He killed my mother as an act of his power—to scare and intimidate us. His result is the exact opposite. If I ever get the chance to lay hands on that fiendish beast, he will wish he never entered this world." I turn and pin Sir Wellington with my gaze. "And believe me, I will."

The breeze whisks through his blond hair and ruffles his leather vest. "That hatred will make you sick."

I puff out air. Who is he to tell me that? Pain tightens my fingers as I grip my bow harder. "If you wish to stay on my good side, you had better watch your words very, very carefully."

He tilts his chin. "You've become weak."

I stare at him. Weak is far from any word I would use to describe myself at the moment.

"Excuse me?" I slap my bow to my side.

"Your anger. The hate you're feeling. It's weakening you."

I whirl and clutch another arrow. I pull back so hard that when I release, the arrow races over the target and far off into the nearby wood.

"You don't realize what hate can do to you, Princess Lorelle." I hear him scuff a foot over the ground. "It will capture you, blind you. You'll be like a sightless person who wanders in the dark, arms always outstretched but never touching anything."

"Really?" My words spark with sarcasm. "If you go around, always afraid to hate, you'll become a pitiful madman."

He crosses his arms over his chest. "I disagree with you completely."

Heat burns my cheeks, hotter than the sun beating down above us. This man is foolish to contradict me.

"Are you calling me dumb, Sir Wellington?"

"I never said any such thing. I merely contradicted you." He moves nearer, his face a hand's breadth away. "Hate forbids us to forgive. Forgiveness brings peace, joy, and strength as almost nothing else can. If we choose to hate, if we refuse to forgive, we will only experience pain and grief."

I lower my bow and stare into the distance. A hawk, his black feathers gleaming, swoops down and perches on the field's target.

"I don't know if you've forgotten, Your Highness, but my father was killed right beside your mother."

My throat tightens as his words hit me.

"I was as close to my father as any son could ever be. He was absolutely everything to me. Since my mother died when I was seven, we grew up extremely dependent on each other. Losing him devastates me. Initially complete hate and want of revenge took control of me." I hear his boot crunch a rock. "That's when I had to choose to forgive King Maurice. It felt impossible, but once I finally succeeded, a flow of peace surrounded me—a peace that nothing can or ever could replace."

Peace. I have longed for peace and contentment my whole life. My failure in the search of it always tortures me, and envy for anyone who has it always sneers at me. Could this be what I am looking for—?

My mind snaps shut. "Sir Wellington," I declare, turning to him, "your beliefs are childish."

"Really?" He smiles, and my effort to intimidate and embarrass him crumbles into a million tiny pieces.

I turn and look out ahead of me as the heat again rushes to my cheeks, stinging like my hands do from rubbing my bow too hard. The servant shifts his stance next to the target. His hands fold awkwardly around each other as my stare hits him.

I flick a curl from my face. "You are dismissed," I tell the servant. He nods and heads for the mansion. As the door shuts behind him, I draw my gaze back to Sir Wellington. "Forgiveness. Is that the source that you're telling me brings complete joy and contentment?" I cock my head, lowering my bow.

"Close." That smiling, all-knowing look that declares he knows one rich secret comes into his eyes. "God is the source."

I smirk. "God. Really." I readjust the position of the bow in my hand. "I'm surprised at you."

"Why?"

"I didn't think a man such as you would stoop to such a low belief."

"You call it low. Why is that, may I ask?"

I take a step closer to him, standing so that we are evenly in front of each other. "Leave God to the bishop, Sir Wellington."

He tilts his chin. "What makes you so opposed to God?"

His breath brushes over my face. "Well, he allowed my mother to die by the ruthless hand of a murderer, didn't he?" I swallow as my throat tenses again. King Maurice has already scarred our family with death. When will he have enough?

Sir Wellington pauses for a moment, yet the confidence doesn't leave his eyes. "You depended on your mother, didn't you? She was everything to you. Your strength, joy, peace, nourishment ..."

I roll my lips, pressing them against each other so hard pain results. "Of course. She was my mother."

He takes a step closer to me. "Now that she is gone, maybe it's time you realize God is the one on whom you can truly depend, the one who gives endless supplies of true joy, peace, strength, comfort, and love."

I again stop. That is almost exactly what Lady Angelet told me two days before. I shift my stance. "What makes you so sure your God is completely and truly dependable?"

"Because His Word says so." His simple answer hangs in the air. His words have become like light clouds—beautiful and free.

"The Bible." I raise my chin and cross my arms, letting my bow hang from the crease in my elbow. "And you believe that?"

"Why shouldn't I? It has stood unshakably for thousands of years. No one can prove it to be incorrect." He pulls a loose strand of blond hair from his eye. "It's the only book in the world that offers eternal life."

"You believe that is what the Bible offers?"

A smile lights his face. "Verse sixteen, chapter three in the book of John, says, 'For God so loved the world that He gave His one and only son, that whosoever believes in Him will not perish but have everlasting life.'"

The words twirl round and round in my head. I shift my feet again.

He pulls on his sleeve. "God sent His one and only son, Jesus, to die on the cross for every sin we have ever committed and ever will commit. Jesus was completely innocent but betrayed and misunderstood. He died so we wouldn't have to. Our prices of sin were so great and so terrible, yet He decided to take the punishment for us. And as He died at the ruthless hands of murderers, He asked His father to forgive His killers."

I swallow. Something is pricking my heart. No, not pricking—asking.

I've had enough. I pull the quiver from my back and set the bow down. "Thank you, Sir Wellington. If you'll excuse me, I've had as much of this fresh air as I want and will retreat to inside."

And with that I rush off, my cheeks flaming and my heart pounding.

My hands brush against my dress as I walk down the hallway, my footsteps clicking against the silver marble floors in the empty silence. A breath of breeze blows onto my body as I walk past the entrance to a balcony. Turning, I stop and let it play with my hair. The moon glistens in the sky, bathing everything in an elegant, white light. Beneath it stands Lady Angelet, her hair flowing out behind her, stirred by the same breeze.

As I walk toward her, she turns and says, "Your Highness." She lowers in a curtsy.

Shame lurches in me. "Oh, please don't." I scarcely believe the words are mine. "I prefer Lorelle from you."

She arises and smiles, her eyes sparkling. "Very well, Lorelle. I would be honored then if you would refer to me as Angelet."

I smile and nod, resting my arms on the railing. A sigh slips from my lips.

She moves her face slightly toward me. "How have you been doing?"

I look her in the eye. "I-I was thinking about what you said a few days ago."

"And?"

I rub my hands on the cold marble railing. "Well, Sir Wellington just told me the exact same thing this afternoon."

She raises her head toward the moon. "I see. Hearing someone else say it has sparked your attention a little more, hasn't it?"

I nod and turn to the midnight sky, the beauty close enough to wrap around me if the stars aren't pinning it back. "He said we can be … we can be truly dependent on God."

"Yes." She straightens her arms, leaning onto the railing. "He is exactly right. God wants us to tell Him everything. He wants us to look at Him as our friend. He wants to know every little detail about our lives—every disappointment, hope, sorrow, dream—everything."

I look toward her. "Is He your best friend?"

A glow of a smile appears on her face. "He most certainly is. He's my confidant, my rock, my shelter, my strength, my peace … I find my contentment in Him."

I turn back toward the sky again. Peace. Contentment. Those words always nag me. Listening to her, they seem the easiest things to find in the world.

"Really?" My voice hushes to a whisper. Something, though I don't know what, is slowly seeping in.

"Really." Her voice swirls in the air, soft as the moonlight around us.

"Sir Wellington also said something about eternal life. Meaning heaven, I would think."

"You are correct." She runs her fingers through her hair that is blowing in the night wind. "If we confess our sins, the Bible says, 'He is faithful and just and will forgive us our sins and purify us from all unrighteousness.' Most importantly, if we commit our lives to Him, He grants us eternal life."

Those words spin around in my ears. "You make it all sound so easy. Peace, contentment, eternal life—you act like you can possess them with one swift grasp."

"That's because you can."

My heart seems to stand still. *Can.*

"Just pray. Realize you're a sinner. Realize you need forgiveness. And realize God is the source."

A misty haze envelops me.

"Talk to Him, Lorelle. Talk to Him."

And she is gone.

CHAPTER 7

Someone knocks on my door, and I cross the room to answer
it. Sir Wellington tips his head.

"Hello," I say, letting go of the door.

"Hello," he replies. "I was wondering, Your Highness, if you
would care to walk the estate's gardens with me?"

I move my head back, surprised. "Let me fetch my cloak."

I turn and walk to my closet. Why on earth did I just say
that? But then I realize I'm smiling. Somehow, from somewhere,
a strange excitement tingles in my chest.

Maybe this will be good for me, another something to distract
me from my mother. I grab the cloak and cross back to him,
throwing it around my shoulders. As I begin to tie it, he reaches in
and secures it for me, his fingers brushing my neck. He then offers
his arm, and I curl mine in his. We walk down the long staircase.

A warm breeze wraps around me as we step outside to the
gardens. The sweet scents of all the flowers swirled into one fill
the air. A bluebird hops to a lower branch of a nearby tree. Colors
of soft pink and red, bright yellow and orange, and gentle purple
and white splash over the grounds, flecked by the green stems.
Thick bushes are scattered here and there, and stone paths weave
throughout the flora.

"I had no idea these gardens were so beautiful," I say, our
footsteps crunching over the pebbles of a path. "I've never been
here before."

"I came here for the first time years ago." He kicks a larger stone out of my way. "I wanted to bring you here."

I grin and look up toward the cloudless sky. Somehow my grief doesn't feel as heavy today. I find myself actually enjoying the beauty around me.

I turn my face toward him. "When did you first come here?"

"When I was seven. Julinar is where I trained to be a knight. I traveled here only weeks after my mother died."

"Really?" I brush some hair out of my eyes. "So is Julinar like a second home to you?"

"You could say that," he replies, the wind rippling through his white blouse.

Pulling me toward a large weeping willow, he brushes the branches aside with his free arm, creating an entryway. I gasp as we slip inside. A perfect circle filled with soft gold and green light awaits us. The leaves swish back together as he brings me to the trunk.

"Beautiful, isn't it?" he says.

I run my hand over the tree's bark then watch the wind ripple through the foliage. "It's perfect. A perfect hideaway."

He grins and leans against the wood. "Whenever there's something on my mind or I'm feeling overwhelmed, I always try to find a quiet spot like this to come and breathe. It's so peaceful."

I nod and rest my back next to his. "When I was younger and I was frustrated, I would always climb a tree."

He laughs. "Climb a tree?"

"Yes! I would sneak out, run into the woods, and climb up into a tree." I lean my head back as a breeze runs through my hair. "There I somehow felt the safest. All alone, far away from anybody else. Just me and the woods."

Sir Wellington picks off a piece of bark. "Would anybody come and find you?"

"Eventually, yes. One time when soldiers found me, I wouldn't come down. They had to force me."

"What had been bothering you?"

I swallow, looking down at a stray leaf flitting around on the ground. "It was nothing."

For a minute, the only sound is the wind ruffling the leaves. "I remember when my mother died," he says, his voice breaking the quiet.

I turn and look at him.

"I ran to the kitchen and shut myself in the pantry. To my seven-year-old mind, it was the perfect hideaway."

"How long did you stay there?"

He watches a squirrel scurry along a branch above us. "Hours. Eventually I cried myself to sleep. I woke up to the cook shaking me awake. She picked me up in her big arms and brought me to my father."

I pull on one of my curls. "You were so young."

He smiles sadly and nods. "Not a day hasn't gone by where I haven't thought of her."

I twist my fingers together. "I know I'll think of my mother every day for the rest of my life."

"That way they never really leave."

A small smile pulls my lips. His hand slips into mine, and he pulls me from the tree and through the drapery of leaves, back into the full sunshine again. My cloak presses on my shoulders, heavy from the heat. Tugging at the strings, I let it slip from my back.

"Here," Sir Wellington says as he grasps it and swings it over his shoulder. He then leads me along another pebble path amid pink and red roses.

"Can I bring you here again tomorrow?" he suddenly asks.

I turn my head just enough so that I can barely look at him, the same excitement tingling again in my chest. "Yes, you may."

Bending down, he plucks a deep red rose, and then, facing me, he gently secures it in my hair.

I look up at him, cocking my head. "Do you believe thorns produce roses or roses produce thorns?"

Grinning, he brushes a loose curl away from my forehead. "I think it's thorns that produce roses. Usually pain can create something beautiful."

———◄○►———

I slam the door shut behind me and slump to the floor. Discouragement washes over me like an icy-cold wave. Will I ever get home?

Rubbing my temples, I lift my head and stare out the window. Lord Richard Williams intends to leave this afternoon, the two weeks since he arrived enough time for his selected tasks in Julinar to be fulfilled. I planned—assumed, rather—that I would be going with him, yet when I stated this, he informed me it was not yet safe for me to return. Nothing I could say would change his mind.

Pulling myself up, I walk to the window and lean my forehead against the cool glass, watching ships sway in the water in Kingston's Harbor. My shoulders twitch, and my dress hangs on me like a blanket. My head throbs.

I rub my hands over my face. Crossing to my door, I open it and slip out. No one familiar catches my eye, so I retreat down the steps and creep to the back exit. Guards, their faces a screen of blankness, stand beside the doors and hardly move a muscle when I appear.

"Open these doors immediately."

The doors crash open. I wince at the loud result. Did anyone hear?

As they bow, I steal out the door and stop when I hear the doors shut behind me. A sweet breeze swirls around me, lifting my hair and filling my lungs. I close my eyes and breathe. This is what I need.

The castle's expanse of land stretches before me. Privacy. Freedom. My feet itch. I let them loose and run toward the woods. Oh, the feel of the wind rushing into my face, the world speeding past me. I love it. Nothing can release tension in my chest like running.

I hike up my skirts and quicken my pace, my hair flying out behind me. Leaves scamper from my feet as I press further into the wood. I lift my head and glue my gaze ahead of me. Miles and miles of trees topped with crowns of leaves stretch as far as I can see, like a whole different world inching closer with every step I take. If I can just keep running and running, I could flee and forget the world that holds me now. Forget the way it locks me in pain, uncertainty, and separation. Forget the way it steals my hope, my love, my security.

My eyes burn. Hauntingly familiar laughter flows past my ears, and the memory of loving blue eyes flashes before me. Why was she taken? Why did the world rip her so mercilessly from me? She didn't just die—she was *killed*, murdered in a tunnel. My throat squeezes. I slow to a walk and lean against a tree, suddenly exhausted. The burning behind my eyes increases.

I blink and lift my head to the sky. It is so vast, so sure. How can something so beautiful cover such a world of hate?

I look back to the direction from which I came. The stink of sorrow grips my new home. Everywhere I turn, a memory of her death pounces on me. Every person seems to hold something related. I hate it there.

If only I could run and never come back. If only I could find a new place where hurt and sorrow doesn't exist, a place where I wouldn't have to shiver through the night, wondering what the morning held or if the morning would even come.

I push from the tree and press on, running against the cool wind. My heart shrivels into a knot of longing and loneliness. I suck in the fresh air, letting it fill my lungs again, and lift my head higher.

My legs fly over the ground as I run faster and faster, my hands clenched into fists. The trees speed past me; the world speeds past me. My mind races with it as I keep my feet flying. I reach down to hike up my skirt when my foot rams into a log, hurling me to the ground. Sticks and rocks jag my body as I reel faster and faster down a sloping hill. Leaves and dust fly into my eyes and mouth. Flashes of green and brown whirl around me until, at last, I thud into a tree.

Squinting against the pain, I lift my head and rub off the dust and leaves. A hut, thirty yards or so from me, squats against a sheltering copse of a towering birch. The faint, familiar smell of salt wafts into my nose. Have I really run so far that I am near the sea? By the looks of the scraggy building, I guess the shack belongs to a fisherman.

A creaking snaps my attention to the door. It opens, and a man steps out. A young, shaven face peers from beneath thick brown hair, and muscle bulges from beneath clothes clean of any tear or filth. Interesting for a fisherman.

When he turns my way, his eyes shoot wide. "Madam! Are you hurt?"

I pull myself to my feet, flicking away leaves and smoothing my dress. "I'm fine, thank you. Forgive me for so rudely intruding."

Twigs crunch under his feet as he hurries closer to me. "Can I help you with anything?"

"Oh, no, please." Embarrassment burns my cheeks. How more ridiculous can I look? A young lady, out by herself, falling down a hill? I clear my throat. "I will be on my way. Thank you."

His voice stops me as I turn to leave. "Begging your pardon, but do I have the honor of addressing the princess of Aundria?"

Wonderful. Now it's a princess rolling down a hill.

I turn back to him, tilting my head. "You do."

He rubs his hands together. "I am honored, Your Highness."

His tone rises. Doubt tickles my chest, but I nod in acknowledgement of his greeting.

He inches closer, his mouth opened to speak. The realization of how unsafe I am drops on me. Alone, out in the thick of the wood, with no escort or means of transportation except my own feet … I swallow.

"To what do I owe this incredible honor?" He sinks to his knees on the ground.

"Nothing, my good man. Thank you."

45

I spin around to leave when a hand rams into my face. I stumble backward as an arm thick as iron clenches my neck. I fling my feet and fists, gagging and coughing, but two hands grab my arms and yank, twisting them behind my back. Two more bind me with a rope. Four hands. Two men.

I kick my feet, my desperate moans behind the hand increasing. A gag snakes across my face, stealing my breath.

"Keep her still!" the first man orders.

"She's kicking enough to make anyone go mad!" a second voice retorts.

"Here, give her to me," a third voice commands.

Two giant hands grab me and thrust me to the ground. I wince, but no scream can filter through the gag. Lying on the dirt, I am finally able, in the short second, to look at the men. The first man, the fisherman, towers over the second man but seems to shrink under the glare of the third.

Muscle bulks from the tallest. My dread rockets when he saunters toward me. In an instant, he grips his arms around me and begins dragging me toward the hut, the other two following. I squirm and flail again, but he tightens his grip so securely I can hardly breathe. I get my legs loose and hit him.

"Good Lord! I didn't expect a female to be so feisty." He takes his fist and knocks my head. "Keep still, you hear me?"

The throbbing in my head immediately causes me to stop flailing. My eyes squeeze shut as I try to block out the pounding pain, but at the scraping of the door, they fly open again.

Their footsteps clunking on the old wooden floor, they drag me through the hut. The one holding me pulls me to a small door at the back of the hut's one room and thrusts it open. He puts me inside, and I'm able to turn and look at him. A deep laugh rumbles from his lips.

"Thank you for being so kind, missy. You saved us a trip to your mansion."

The door slams shut. My breaths snake out ragged and sharp, while disbelief raps through me. I slump against the wall, a heavy stupor clouding me, and pull my gaze around the room. The dim light seeping under the door barely gives the small space enough light. Shelves line the walls on each side of me. Green, red, and clear bottles litter the scuffed wood. Rum.

My head lightens. Gritting my teeth, I twist and jerk against the ropes. I am now a prisoner? Anger chokes my throat. The gag glues my lips to my teeth. I rub my mouth against the wall. Splinters dig into my chin, and the wood scrapes against my skin until it feels like a piece of raw meat.

The gag finally falls to my neck. Breath freely rushes through me as I lean my head back.

My stomach sickens as my anger shrinks beneath new fear. Horrors of what could happen to me flash across my mind. My throat turns to sawdust. I dig my hands into the wall, sawing up and down over the wood until the ropes loosen. Again. I force all my energy into the rubbing, my teeth clenching. Up, down. Up, down. Harder, harder, until the ropes fall down my back.

Flinging my arms in front of me, I jump to my feet and press my hands against the door. Solid. I glue my ear against it. Silence. I move my fingers to the knob and shake with all my might, resulting in only burning skin.

My teeth sinking into my lip, I step to the wall on the other side. I suck in a breath and hurl myself against the door. It rattles in the frame, laughing at me.

I step back and ram into it a second time. My shoulder throbs in protest.

Quiet settles down again. I stare at the door, discouragement and anger rushing over me. Scanning the room, I search for any kind of window, any opening.

Nothing.

I run my hands over the wall, patting and feeling every inch. Nothing.

I turn to the shelves, shoving aside bottles and patting the wood. My sigh fills the silence. No secret compartment, no key, nothing from which to glean the slightest bit of hope. I sink to the floor, finally swallowing my predicament. All I can do is wait.

———◁◦▷———

A door slams. I shoot my eyes open, sleep charging off. Footsteps pound across the floor outside my prison.

The door to my room swings open. I scramble to my feet when the biggest of the men steps in and grabs me. I twist and reach for the door, but he pulls me back and clamps my arms to my sides. Grabbing the rope on the floor, he fastens it around me. My breath whisks away as my stomach clenches beneath the pressure. A gag covers my mouth.

Light stabs my eyes as he drags me through the doorway. I blink and flick my gaze across the room, letting my surroundings register. Morning sunlight needles into my eyes, rushing through the hut's open door.

The door.

I fling my legs at the man. A groan of surprise slips from his mouth, but he silences any attempt at escape as he hurls me to the ground.

"We'll not have anymore of that!" he snarls, securing his grip on me.

We leave the hut behind us and eventually reach the top of a cliff. My breath catches in my throat.

The men are bringing me down an uncomfortably narrow path on the side of a cliff. Below us, a boat sits beached in a bay sheltered by boulders. The cliffs almost completely surround the water. When I turn my head, I notice a ship—hardly detectable—miles away.

Escape. I have to escape, or I will never come back here. And time is running out.

I start to twist my body when the throbbing rockets in my head and the ropes rub against me, holding me inside their cage. I can barely move.

As we enter the beach, I scan the cliffs. On the far side, at the very top, a figure moves. I gulp in a breath. I don't care who the person is. He's my only chance.

I begin kicking, flailing, twisting. Within seconds I succeed in sliding the gag from my face. I open my mouth and scream at the top of my lungs.

The surprise that results from my outburst loosens the men's grasp on me. I lung forward, my feet barely missing entangling each other, and race across the beach.

"Help! Help me!"

The figure turns. Within an instant, he is pounding down the beach. I pick up speed, my eyes glued to him, and prepare for another scream when a hand slams over my face and two bodies hurl themselves on top of me.

I gasp, my legs sprawling over the sand as the men drag me toward the boat.

"He's coming. Get her into the boat now!"

My panic escalates as the boat comes nearer and nearer. I fight with everything in my body, trying to stall until the stranger can reach me. As I tear my face away from the giant's hand and thrust my head around, my heart stops. Sir Wellington races across the beach.

The giant grabs me and pulls me forward, but I break away from his clasp and run to the side of the boat. I'm curling my leg over the side when he catches my dress and yanks me back. Just as he drags me to the back of the boat, the sound of the duelers' fighting is silenced. We both spin our heads around.

The short man, bloody and crumpled, falls to the ground. Sir Wellington pulls his sword free and jumps to the next man. As the crash of metal splits the air, the giant drags me onto the boat, grunting and cursing. The ropes around my arms fall to my waist. He pushes me onto a crate, forces another rope around my legs, then pins me to the ground.

My gaze shoots back to the duelers. Sir Wellington feints left, and the man slits the air with his sword. Swinging it back around, the man slices downward when Sir Wellington reaches

49

up and blocks it, the clash piercing my ears. Sir Wellington spins around, parrying another blow, and then crashes his sword into his enemy's. They hold for a minute, swords pitted against each other, each man struggling to stand against the other's weight. Sir Wellington's opponent jumps back, catching Sir Wellington off guard. Sir Wellington stumbles, and the man thrusts his sword into Sir Wellington's side. As Sir Wellington collapses, a scream rips from my throat.

"No! Please! No!"

"Keep her silent!" The dueler sloshes through the water and jumps into the boat. "She'll have soldiers coming!"

The giant jumps from me and grabs an oar. With three long pulls, he sends the boat skidding through the water. My head still spinning, I clasp the side of the boat, pulling myself upward until I can see the beach. A pool of blood surrounds the motionless Sir Wellington. Screams break through my lips before I can even think. I curl over the side and reach forward when a hand clutches my throat and throws me back. My head rams against something solid.

"Get her silent!" The words seem thousands of miles away.

"There's nothing for a gag."

"Here, take this. Do it. Now!"

I drag my head up and see a rusted metal anchor in the hand of the giant. I try to scramble away, but in the next second everything goes black.

CHAPTER 8

A faint, eerie light seeps through my eyelids. I blink, barely awake. Pain throbs through my temples. I groan and clutch my head. Like feet stomping on me, the pain is almost unbearable.

I loosen my grip on my head. There's some rocking movement beneath me—the same type of movement I noticed during my first day away from home.

I am on a ship.

Fear and uncertainty drizzle over me like countless cold raindrops. Right below the ceiling, dim light seeps through a window no larger than the size of a book. I look around. Minus the light, a room of complete black meets my gaze. Nothing is in it except myself, and I practically take up the whole room.

Where on earth am I? Where am I going? Looking down at my arms, I see bruises, dried blood, and scars covering my skin. Soreness grips my body, imprisoning every movement. I lift my hand to the raw spot on my head. My fingers slip into a gash.

How did this all happen? How was I so foolish and naive? And why on earth didn't I tell anybody where I was going?

My heart reels. Sir Wellington.

Tears sting my cheeks. I move my hand to swipe them away but only succeed in crumpling over in pain. Sir Wellington is dead. And all the blame belongs to me.

An icy fear like I have never felt before clutches me, sending shivers through my body. I wrap trembling arms around myself, my teeth chattering while my thoughts race to my home—to Aundria—to safety.

The door swings open, barely missing my feet. The giant reaches down and wraps his huge hands around my arms. Lifting me up, a blast of sea air swooshes in as he brings me out of the room.

Overhead, the black sky looms like a claw. Sailors hustle around on the main deck. Stopping, my captor takes his hand and runs it through his knot of hair. I lift my head and stare around me. A small ship with an Alandarin flag bobs on the black water. My gaze shifts upward. Only yards away, on the shore, a castle towers over everything. A large Alandarin flag waves from the highest point. The sign of utmost hatred. My jaw tightens.

A blast of cold wind rushes over me. I shiver. The murkiness sends chills racing up and down my body. Soldiers stand guard everywhere I look, and a large, muddy moat surrounds the entire palace. An iron fence stands as the final defense, its top jagged with spikes.

I shake my head against the breeze. Hunger claws at my stomach. As my insides seem to cramp into a ball, my mother's last words to me come flooding back. I have to stay strong for her and my country.

The ship rams against the dock. The giant drags me to the gangplank and leads me across.

"Bourne," a low voice rasps.

My oppressor turns and lifts a hand in greeting. "Sir Cardon."

A man steps out of the shadows. Dark brown hair covers his scalp, and a curled mustache and beard trim his face. Wrinkles furrow the skin around his gleaming gray eyes. Hard, set lines dent the rest of his face, and a round, gold earring hangs from his left ear. Uneasiness slithers into me just looking at him.

He stops in front of me. "So this must be the princess, eh?" A low smirk slides from his lips. "You sure don't look much like royalty. And that's a nice little gash you've got there." The gray eyes move to the face above me. "Good work, Bourne. I trust they got her without much trouble." His icy gaze shifts again to me, a ghost of a smile on his face. "We don't want her running away now, do we? Bourne, bind and gag her."

"Yes, sir." My captor turns to one of the sailors. "Bring me a rope."

When the sailor comes running and hands him the rope, he kneels to the ground. Thrusting my hands behind my back, he twists them with the rope and then curls the rest around my upper body.

I hold in a groan. Finished securing me, he picks me up with one arm and drags me away from the port, the soldiers following us. The gate entrance soon looms before us. Immediately the soldiers swing the huge iron slabs open and allow us to enter. A wide, wooden bridge stretches over the moat, and we hurry across it, but instead of entering through the main gate, we turn and circle the castle to the back. A metal door stands like a mountain in the gray wall. Soldiers turn the lock and drag it open, revealing a long, descending tunnel.

We plunge into it. The cold increases, turning my blood to ice. I try to shift my position, hoping to breathe easier, but the man's arm holds me like an iron bar. One of the soldiers grabs a lantern hanging on the wall and strikes a match to it, throwing light into the darkness.

As we descend deeper and deeper, moans, faint and muffled, drift to my ears. My throat tenses. I begin shaking again, and I can't tell if it's from cold or fear.

A small door in the stone wall appears from the shadows. A soldier pulls it open, and the shinning glint of keys meets my eyes. He grasps one, and we continue our hike.

Metal bars rising up from the dirt catch my attention. Prison cells.

"This one will do." A soldier unlocks one of the doors and swings it open. My captor drags me inside and throws me to the ground. In a moment the ropes have been torn from me.

"Make yourself at home," his deep voice booms, followed by a low laugh. He reaches down next to me, a silver bottle in hand, and thrusts it against my mouth. Water spills onto my tongue and slides down my throat. I grasp the bottle and drink, and then he tears it away from me. The door slams and locks.

Shaking, I position myself again the wall, scrunching my face in pain. What are they going to do with me? King Maurice has already brought enough death into my family. Will he now wrap his slimy fingers around my neck and squeeze the life from me too? I could be down in this cell for years. I could starve. Or—

Ransom.

They will probably hold me for ransom. But for how long? And when will the people back at the Julinarin estate notice my absence? And Sir Wellington's?

Sir Wellington. Probably still lying alone on the beach, dead.

I let my head drop against the wall behind me.

Minutes pass. Or hours. I have no idea.

The sound of a door being unlocked jerks me awake. Two soldiers push the door open, and one comes inside, raises me to my feet, and leads me out of the cell.

I look up, searching for light that signals the end of the tunnel. Even though I have no idea where they are taking me, escaping that icebox of a prison warms me.

More faint moans drift past us as we move across the dirt. A drop of water splashes on my head from the ceiling and soaks my scalp as the sharp smell of dirt mixed with water and waste stings my nose. Glinting bars of metal flash beside me as we make our way through the dark. A thin mist hangs in the air, sinking into my skin and settling into my blood.

Stopping beside a door hidden in the wall, one of the soldiers slides a key into the rusting lock and swings it open, the grating sound digging into my ears. We walk through and travel up the staircase inside. Another door greets us at the top. The soldiers push it open, and we slip through.

A dimly lit hallway meets my gaze. Gray stone still covers the walls and floor, but the faint glow of a single lantern fastened to a hook softens the atmosphere. We only take one step when my knees buckle. Pain sloshes through my head as the soldiers clench my arms and jerk me up. My feet drag like bricks as we continue our hike.

Soon a long, elaborate hallway stretches before us. Large candles hang on every wall, along with various suits of knights' armor and weapons.

The throne room. We must be near the throne room.

When we reach the doors, servants grasp the handles and haul them open. A stream of red spills from the doors to a gilt chair. A throne.

My eyes climb from the chair's feet to the chair's master. I curl my fists. Hate burns in my chest as heat inflames every part of my body.

The moment the guards drag me through the doors, a hush freezes the room. Hundreds of eyes as cold as the dead of winter glue themselves to me.

When we reach the king, the soldiers release their grip on me and thrust me to the floor. As I pull myself to my knees, I hear the deep, mocking voice boom above me.

"Well, well, well! Princess Lorelle, thank you for being so punctual. We do appreciate it."

I lift my head and stare into King Maurice's eyes. The exact same spark of hatred and ice that I first saw years ago still glints in them. Hard lines now carve themselves into his face. Thinning hair the color of mud sticks out from beneath the adornment that marks his power.

Flames of hatred scourge my chest. The fire spreads and simmers in my stomach then down my legs to my toes. It sizzles through my arms, to my fingers, trembling at my fingertips. It rushes up my neck, burning my throat, and stings behind my eyes. The same scream I heard when I first laid eyes on him years ago echoes in my head.

The wet lips part. "After talking with my men, I learned you truly made your capture easy for them." His eyes move to the gash at my temple. "I do see, though, that you put up a little fight.

Well, Princess, now that you are in our hands, your father just may soon be too. He cares the world about you." He leans farther out of his chair and closer to me. "He would do anything for you."

My chest tightens.

"So you, my dear, are remaining here until your father does what I wish for him to do to free you." His eyes shine with savage delight. He sticks his nose even closer to me and glazes his words with ice. "You had better hope the love your father had for you hasn't faded away in the time you've been gone." His eyes drift to the soldiers standing above me. "Take her away."

I grit my teeth as the soldiers drag me from the room, the hate in my body pumping my heart so fast it almost hurts to breathe. I use their grip to pull myself up, doing my best to walk instead of just letting them drag me. I blink my eyes. The throbbing in my head has picked up speed.

At the cell door, my knees again buckle from the trek. Heaviness hangs over my body like a thundercloud. I let my head fall against one of the soldier's arms as heat scorches my skin and blood.

After they bring me inside my cell, one soldier kneels down and unties me. Our eyes meet before he stands up. His face softens for a moment, and then he's gone, and I'm locked in the black again. Lying there in the dark, alone and quiet, sweat trickles down my face and back.

A fever. Wonderful.

The moans groan again in the distance. I shudder. How many other prisoners are around me?

My eyes squeeze shut as I press my hands against my head.

How on earth did they know I was in Julinar? No one saw me escape ... I groan. The Alandarin ship we spotted on our way to Julinar—they must have seen me and guessed my destination.

I sink against the wall, discouragement sweeping over me. My only hope is that King Maurice will contact my father quickly and that my father will respond as quickly. Maybe, maybe ...

Minutes pass. Hours. Time swims into a blur. Do these hours turn into a day? Another day? Heat like fire burns in my throat.

A pounding in my chest splits my breathing. My mind tries to unravel itself out of the tangle I'm becoming trapped in, but even the stone walls in front of me are beginning to contort into a mesh of twisting black.

A grating screech slices the air as the prison door swings open. Two dark figures walk toward me. I shrink against the thought of another attack—another large hand locking around me, another fist finding a home against my head. Desperate for escape, I thrash against the stones with what little energy I have, trying to move farther from those figures ... those figures ... no, no ... so thirsty, so hungry, leave me alone ...

A hand touches my cheek, as two others clasp my slashing hands. I moan and shake my head, flinching at each touch.

"Miss, miss ..."

The words press against me.

"Miss, it's all right. Please, calm ..."

My ears perk. The voice ... it doesn't drip with hatred and threat.

"Miss, here. Here. Open your lips. There ..."

The feel of metal cools my lips, and water spills into my mouth. Water. I seize the cup and let it rush in, gulping it down and letting it smooth my grated tongue and throat.

"Heavens, she's thin. Hand me the bowl."

My body shakes from fatigue. Feeling somewhat safer, I slump against the wall. I try to open my eyes, but my head throbs, and my stomach claws, and—

Thick, warm liquid slips through my lips and trickles to my stomach, warming every bit of me. "There, there. That's it. A little more."

The clawing in my stomach relaxes as more of the liquid spills into it. I sip and swallow, sip and swallow, my fingers unclenching as the pain in my body eases.

A hand touches my forehead. "Just as I thought. Three days since she's eaten, and two days in this rathole of a dungeon. She's burning with fever."

I hear water trickling, and then a cool, damp cloth presses against my forehead. Another warmer, thicker cloth soothes the raw skin on the side of my head. I wince but only for a second as whatever lies in the cloth begins to relieve the pain.

"It's not as deep as it could be. A bit of medicine for the infection, a few bandages, and we'll have this gash under control."

"They must have hit her with a rock or something," a different voice says.

Odd sounds like bottles clicking, caps twisting, and liquid trickling meets my ears. Seconds later a cold spoon eases itself between my lips.

"Open up for me, miss. There."

A sharp-tasting liquid splatters my tongue and finds its way down my throat. I gulp. Another few seconds and two hands wrap a cloth around my head, gently securing it. A blanket settles across my shoulders. The clinking of bowls, bottles, and spoons swirl around my ears. A door opens and shuts, a key twists in a lock, and then silence fills the room.

I open my eyes and stare at the cell door, clearly making out the bars stretching to the ceiling. Pulling the blanket tighter around me, I lift my head and breathe in. Only darkness appears beyond my cell door. The large lock amid the bars glints. Who were those people?

Water droplets from the walls crawl through my dress to my skin. I shiver and draw my knees to my chest, shaking from cold yet burning with heat. Will my life ever return to normal again? Will things ever be as they were?

Memories of home flood back. The wonderful joy my mother, father, and I shared had been ripped from us by the war—ripped by the very person that kept me locked in this pit. Never again could I sense that security, laugh with that joy, feel my mother's arms around me ... Alandar had as tight a clutch on me, my fate, and any reunion with my father as a hundred pairs of shackles.

Father, if only you could see your daughter now. My heart wrenches. Shame churns in my stomach. Why am I so awful?

Hardly a care for anyone else. Just me. Everything about *me*. Arrogant, conceited, spoiled.

I haven't carried my title appropriately. I am the crown princess of Aundria, yet the way I act lacks the heart and dignity a princess should have. My thoughts have not been on my people and how I could help them, but on me.

I think of Sir Wellington again—his wall of strength and confidence and the joy and peace that never seemed to leave him …

Peace. He struck me as the kind of man that even if life turned and twisted until it fell apart, he could still carry his head high and wear a smile on his face. Why was that? When his father died, he seemed to have something to hold on to. He forgave the murderer who is keeping me locked in this dungeon, trusting in a higher power as I had never seen. He tried to share his hope with me, and I ridiculed him.

And now he is dead, undoubtedly still lying crumpled on the beach, undiscovered. The man who never withered, now lying like a trampled plant.

My mind clicks. God. Was that Sir Wellington's secret, his never-ending strength? He even said it, and I dismissed it.

Where is God now? Why has He allowed this to happen to me? Why did He strip me of absolutely anything to hold on to?

Sir Wellington's words ease themselves into my ears. *"Maybe it's time you realize God is the one on whom you can truly depend."*

I look around the black dungeon. Nothing. No one to confide in. No one to lean on. No one to trust, unless …

My gaze drifts upward to the ceiling and the dark stones held together by thick mortar. How can I hold on to something that I can't even reach out to grasp? Nothing but blackness looms in front of me. Where is God now?

I am here.

My heart stops and then flitters to life again.

I am here.

The burden lifts off my shoulders. Something releases the tension in my chest, brushes away the pain in my head. Something

59

relieves me of my burning heat. Something gently takes a hold of my heart.

A tremendous wave of peace washes over me, drenching me to the bone. Joy rushes in its wake. I push back my shoulders and stare into the gloom ahead of me. The black claws no longer lash out at me.

"God, thank You. Thank You! Jesus, I-I need something to live my life for. Until now, I've only been living my life for myself, and it's done absolutely nothing but rot into a pit inside me."

The darkness has shrunk. The presence is still there.

"God, will You take my life? I give it all to You. Every bit of it. Transform me. Create in me a different person."

I pause as guilt presses in on me. "Jesus, will You please forgive my sin? For being selfish and proud and arrogant—I'm so, so sorry. Will You completely wash me until I'm clean?"

The guilt drowns in another wave of peace. "Jesus, thank You for Your forgiveness—and life. Thank You so much."

Apparently my eyes were shut, for they flit open. I lay my head back against the wall and release a sigh. I have just been given a gift—free. *Free.* And never, never will I take for granted the peace, joy, and strength that has just washed over me. Not even as I sit in a place as cold and unforgiving as a dungeon.

CHAPTER 9

The cell door creaks open, and a middle-aged man and woman enter, a guard shutting the door behind them. My eyes locking on them, I straighten my back against the wall.

The woman kneels down beside me, a bowl and jug of water in her hands. The smell of onions, garlic, and chicken floats into my nose. She sets the bowl in my lap and then gently begins unwrapping my bandage.

"Is there much pain, Your Highness?"

One of King Maurice's servants calling me Your Highness? I look into her eyes, eyes that are deep brown and flecked with soft marks of gold, like tiny pieces of the sun. A bun pulls her chestnut-colored hair out of her face, but a few perfectly-curled wisps have escaped.

"A small throbbing," I answer, looking to the man beside her. A bottle and a cloth rest in his hands while a blanket is draped over his shoulders. His green eyes meet mine, and a few wrinkles circle them as he smiles.

"It's healing well," the woman says as I bring a spoonful of soup to my mouth. The sharp and salty flavor from the onions and garlic soaks my tongue. I roll my lips and chew the tender chicken.

Bunching my used cloth into a ball, she exchanges it for the new one and spreads it out on her lap. Taking the bottle from the man, she sprinkles some of the clear liquid onto the fabric. My gash stings in protest as she wraps it around my head.

A work-roughened hand presses my forehead, but as she then moves it to my cheeks, a softness comes through that reminds me of my mother, gently stroking my hair whenever I was sick in bed.

"Your fever seems to be almost wiped out." She smiles at me, warming me like the soup that is filling my stomach. "You even have a little more color in your cheeks."

As a small smile tugs my lips, the man pulls the blanket from around his shoulders and layers it on top of the other one that lies on me. He secures it around my neck and pats my shoulder.

"This isn't any place for a lady, but we mean to keep you healthy." His lips stretch into a grin, revealing two lines of straight, small teeth.

I look from him to the woman and back to him again. "Thank you."

She wraps the ends of the blankets around my feet. "It's the least we can do. I'm relieved to see you're recovering."

Their concern touches me, letting me feel just a hint of security in the uncertainty around me.

Collecting their things, they rise to their feet and make their way to the cell door. "You can call me Betsy, and this is my husband, Martin." The woman smiles. "We'll be here to make sure you're all right."

I open my mouth to say thank you when the door's hinges groan and a soldier reaches in and ushers them out. The door's slam echoes in the corridor.

———◄○►———

"Your Highness, Your Highness ..."

My shoulders move back and forth as two hands shake them. "Your Highness ..."

Sleep presses on me like a heavy mantle. It almost steals me away again, but I pull my eyes open and blink up at Betsy.

She grins. "You all right?"

I nod my head, curled in my blankets. Grogginess makes talking seem like a feat right now.

She cocks her head at me, still smiling. "Were you dreaming? You were pretty stubborn in waking up."

I furrow my brow. No dreams, no nightmares. I was in such a deep sleep that even my subconscious was silent. The first solid deep sleep I've had in weeks.

"Here." She hands me a bowl of soup as I pull myself up to a sitting position. "I want you to have enough time to eat this before I'm ordered out."

I rub my face and take the spoon from her. Thick cream filled with sweet beef and chunks of celery jerk my taste buds awake.

She studies my wound. "It's been a week, and your gash seems to be doing fine without the bandage. Is the pain gone?"

"Once in a while it will give me a small headache, but it's nothing that isn't manageable," I answer, my mouth full.

"That's to be expected." She smooths out my rumpled blankets. "How has everything else been down here? Have you been warm enough?"

"As warm as I can be this far underground," I reply. "Without these blankets, I'd be frozen. Thank you for making sure I'm so well cared for."

A soft smile appears on her face. "It has been my honor, Your Highness."

I swallow my bite, the same feeling of formality pricking me. My eyes meet hers. "Will you call me Lorelle?"

She folds her hands on her lap, her eyes shining with her gentle smile. "I would be more than happy to." She brushes a finger over a small faded scar on my lower arm. "What's this from?"

I grin, memories splashing back. "I fell out of a tree when I was eight." I stretch my skin, watching the scar turn white, and then ease back into light red again as I let go. "Trees were my little hideaways."

She cocks her head with a grin. "Nature makes for the best hideaways." She nods toward the bowl in my hands. "How's the soup? Filling you up enough?"

I nod, savoring the sweet flavor. "Who cooks this?"

"I do."

I stop eating. "You're the cook?"

Sitting back on her heels, she shakes her head. "Not really. I just help the head cook with making food for some of the other servants and prisoners."

I chew on the beef. "Well, this is delicious. What else do you do?"

"I usually gather most of the food, and many days it is my job to go into town and buy supplies. I've been fortunate to have fairly easy work. Not many servants can boast of the same."

I hand her back the empty bowl. "How long have you worked here?"

Her eyes cloud and wander to the wall beside me. I jump as the prison door swings open and a soldier ducks inside.

She squeezes my hand before she springs up and hurries out of the cell.

———◇———

A scream yanks me awake. I jerk, blinking my eyes open. Am I dreaming? I pull my head from the ground and let the iron bars and black stone walls around me register. Muffled sounds throb and buzz in my head as I move my back to the wall. Are my ears playing tricks on me again?

But when the second shriek comes, any doubt scrambles away.

My heart jumps into a frenzy of pounding. A chorus of screams and yells rise and cut through the air.

I crawl across the dirt floor and lean my head against the cell bars. The yells are coming from behind a wooden door that stands a few yards away from me.

I push against the bars and strain to catch a word, any word.

"Open every room! Search every slave!"

A shiver slices through my body. Slaves? Another round of cries crimps the air.

64

The sound of furniture crashing and wood tearing thickens the mess. Soldiers? What are they doing?

The next new plead throws my heart to my throat. Betsy, the woman who steps into my cell every day, a smile always lighting her face and her friendship always warming my heart.

I tighten my hands around the bars. The trail of those sounds etches itself into my mind. No, no ... I hate it. The cold bars stand solid against my grasps, locking me in.

I inch back toward the farthest corner and dig my fists into my ears, squeezing my eyes shut.

————◄o►————

The cell door rattles as a soldier shakes the key in the lock. The door swings open, and the soldier moves to the side as two people come in. Betsy and Martin. Smiles peek from their faces—faint but still there.

Breath rushes out of me as they walk over to me, the door clanging shut behind them.

"Betsy! Betsy—"

She drops to her knees and brushes her finger against my lips before I can finish. A gash, rimmed by bruises, mars her head.

I lean forward. "Betsy, last night ..."

A soft chuckle slides through her lips as she sets a bowl of soup in my lap. "I'm sure it frightened you." She glances at her husband. "We're all right."

He nods and brushes his hand over my blanket. I look from him to Betsy's brown jewels of eyes. So tired, so worn. Her scream echoes in my head. "W-what happened?"

Blowing out a sigh, she returns my gaze. "Some weapons were stolen sometime yesterday. Slaves were the first suspects."

I've never thought anything of slaves in my life. They are just shadows, appearing when you need them and disappearing when you don't. Like flies, you are able to whisk them away or stomp on them anytime you want.

My eyes flicker to the floor. Now here are two, kneeling beside me, real and alive. They aren't shadows. They are people. Real people.

Betsy's explains further, halting my train of thought. "Soldiers searched every room. Their own weapons were drawn, and they used them to move anyone who got in their way, force anyone out of a bed or a room … not caring about age or if the pain inflicted was in front of loved ones. They tore out boards and broke furniture, searching until they found the weapons."

When she pauses, I raise my gaze back to her face. She is biting her lip, her eyes glued to the floor. "Forgive me," she says. "I have said too much."

I rub my hands over my arms. Pain surfaces as strong as waves in her eyes.

I slip my fingers through her cold ones. "Were the weapons found?"

"In the room next to us," she whispers.

I swallow. No doubt friends who made the wrong choice and paid for it with their lives.

"Betsy, I'm so sorry."

She leans back and lets her eyes drift toward the ceiling. "We'll miss them. But what's done is done."

When my gaze moves from her eyes to her gash, I shudder as all the possibilities of what could have happened to create it race through my head. How did they become slaves? I pull her hand toward me and look at Martin. "How did you ever come to this point?"

He rests his hand on his knee. "The only way a line of slaves can start: kidnapping."

In shock, I open my mouth and ask, "How long ago?"

"We were both twenty-one."

My stomach flips. As my mind swims, Betsy dusts a fresh cloth with a few drops of ointment and gently pats my wound.

I bring my eyes back to her and Martin. Their care and love for me … why do they give it so freely? They could just come in and feed me and leave, without so much as a thought to my wound, my fever, my feelings ...

The words rush out like water. "Why are you doing all this for me?"

She stops patting, her hand midair, and locks her eyes with mine. "Because we are called to love." She pauses. "And you are the daughter of our king."

My heart skips a beat. "Aundrians?"

They both repeat the word: "Aundrians."

"How...?"

"We were visiting friends here and got caught in a raid." The words edge off Martin's tongue like worn commands.

"Were you sold to the king?"

"Yes."

"How long have you been here?"

Betsy's gaze melts, staring into an imaginary land far away. "It's growing on twenty-five years."

I tighten my arms around my stomach, a sweep of guilt and emptiness suddenly rushing over me. Twenty-five years locked in a castle, serving a tyrant of a king against your will. No freedom or independence. Everything stripped to the bone, gone forever.

Suddenly the injustice done to the two people in front of me grabs my heart and twists it. Something. Let me do something.

"Eat."

Martin's voice almost makes me jump. A bowl of soup still sits on my lap, steam curling into my nose. I nod and take a small bite.

As the liquid warms my tongue, I ponder their words. For the first time, I look at the two people in front of me as people of my country, people of my king, people of my father.

Betsy suddenly reaches forward and squeezes my hand. "You will survive. And so will our country."

◄◦►

The footsteps draw closer and closer. I peer into the darkness, letting my teeth sink into my lip. Please not another prisoner. I've seen enough pass by my bars, either shredded to pieces or glued together by blood.

A taste of iron spills onto my tongue. I bit too hard.

A dark shape stops outside the black bars. I straighten my shoulders and stare ahead. The door opens, and five soldiers stream into my cell.

They pull me to my feet and then lead me from the cell, heading toward the entrance of the dungeons.

Soon, we leave the train of pits behind us. Where …?

They lead me through a metal door and down a stone-paved hallway as black as coal. They then stop at one of many metal doors lining the walls. Throwing it open, they push me inside and slam it shut—and then they are gone.

I stare at the door, shock and confusion wrapping around me. I turn to study my new surroundings. Minus the door, wooden planks the color of honey cover every inch of the room. A mattress as thin as paper resting on spindly iron legs creates a bed in one corner, while a hump of blankets lies underneath. Next to it, a table holds a small pile of books and a lantern with matches. Streams of sunlight pour through a window below the ceiling. All else is air.

I walk to the pool of light and let it flood over me. Gold and warmth cover my body as I extend my arms and close my stinging eyes. Light. How long has it been since I have seen full light? I turn to the bed and crawl onto it, ignoring the springs jumping up at me. My joy is short-lived, for moments later, the bolt slides back and the door opens. I ease up on the bed, my eyes glued to the slab of metal. Two figures enter. Betsy and Martin.

As the door is shut and locked behind them, grins almost split their faces. Betsy pulls some lint from her dress's folds. "A little more comfortable, isn't it?"

I let out a laugh of surprise. "What did you two do?"

Her eyes shine. "I mentioned to the jailor you were sick and wounded. With that and the condition of the dungeons, it was decided you would be moved. A dead princess doesn't make for a very valuable hostage."

Martin straightens the pile of books on the table. "Since we were already assigned to you, they moved you into our room."

I stare at them in disbelief.

Betsy sits down on the bed beside me and takes my hand in hers. "This atmosphere will give you a bit more room to recover, don't you think?"

I smile and sink back into the bed's pillow. Squeezing her hand and looking at Martin, I whisper, "Thank you."

———◦———

The huge doors swing open, and the enormous throne room looms before me and the soldiers gripping my arms. They pull me inside and hurl me upon the floor. A zinging pain shoots up my arm. I grind my teeth into my cheek. The past two weeks haven't held a speck of commotion, so why now have I been dragged from my cell so suddenly?

The soldiers back away from me.

"Here she is," says King Maurice. No voice do I hate more than that tyrant's. "Hand me the papers and the money, and she's yours."

She's yours.

The sounds of rustling feet and papers shuffling swarm around me.

"Sign here," a different voice orders.

The scratching of a quill follows, and then the king booms, "Done! Now take her and go."

I look up. King Maurice smiles at me from the throne, his face pinched into a smug knot, holding money and … were those land deeds?

Hands grasp my arms—not pinching and cruel but gentle. Still, I flinch.

I've been sold. I know that much. As what? A slave?

Someone unties my restraints, and the ropes drop next to my side. The hands lift me up. Turning my head, I stare into dark-green eyes.

The eyes lower as the man bows. "Your Highness."

Your Highness. Soldier after soldier stand behind him and two—lords? And the soldier's armor ...their shields ... Aundrian soldiers!

My heart jumps to my throat. All of them bow before me. One offers his arm, and I loop my fingers across it, shock throbbing through me. I'm leaving. Leaving. Never has a word sounded so beautiful in my entire life.

They turn and lead me toward the throne room doors. Am I really going home?

I think of the man behind me, sitting on his throne, boring his eyes into my back. I press my nails into my palm and stare ahead as we leave the room behind us.

Alandarin soldiers join us and escort us to the castle's main doors, which swing open, flushing light and color into my eyes. Stepping out onto the moat's extended bridge, fresh air fills my lungs. Never has the sky looked so blue or the breeze felt so cool. Never have the trees looked so tall or the grass so green. The whole world seems to come alive.

I am free.

As we hurry through the village to the harbor where a Julinarin ship bobs on the water, my thoughts fall on Betsy and Martin. Hopefully they will know I am all right, and hopefully they will realize how much they have done for me. I will never forget them.

My feet itch as we cross to the ship. Not until I step on board do I dare breathe. Safety. I let a wave of relief drench me to the bone.

A tall man walks through the thick of bowed sailors and crosses to me. When he reaches me, he lowers in respect. "Your Highness." After rising and kissing my hand, he continues, "It is a true relief to have you safely with us again. I am Captain Drake Carrington. Your father sent me to release you. He has been beside himself with worry." He takes a step closer to me. "Are you all right, Princess?"

"I am, thank you." I rub my hands together. "Just a bit weary."

"We will get you to Julinar as quickly as we can. Aundria, unfortunately, is still in the process of recovering. It is not yet completely safe for you to return."

I nod. "Thank you, Captain. How is my father?"

"Your father is well. He is very concerned about you, but well."

"And do you know how those at the Julinarin estate fare?" My stomach tightens into a knot. I don't dare ask about Sir Wellington.

He shifts his belt. "They are also well."

My shoulders loosen a little, but the knot in my stomach does not. "Thank you, Captain."

He nods and turns to the sailors on the deck. "Make ready to leave port."

As sailors began rushing to their duties, he motions to the lords behind me. "Thank you, men. We have succeeded. Lord Shoremen, will you please take Princess Lorelle to her room?" His gaze travels back to me. "Someone will be down with you shortly to attend to your needs."

I follow the lord through the dodging sailors to a short flight of stairs. After leading me down it, he brings me to a door near the end of a short hallway. He opens it, bows, and gestures for me to enter.

I walk through the entrance. A small room, very similar to my first quarters on a ship, meets my gaze. A bed sits in one corner, with a tiny table standing next to it. A window plants itself directly above the table. That's all. Yet already it looks like a piece of home.

Walking further into the room, I trace my fingers along the windowsill and gaze at the waves rolling onto the side of the ship below. Those waves will soon take me back to Julinar.

I look back at the lord. "Thank you, Lord Shoremen."

He nods and closes the door. A bottled sigh rushes through my lips. Julinar. Angelet. Lord Harmon. The words dance around in my mind.

Thank You, Lord Jesus. Thank You so much.

And then the knot in my stomach stiffens. Sir Wellington. I rub my face in my hands and look through my fingers out the window. Guilt pulls the knot tighter, making me want to get sick. I swallow. I don't think that guilt will ever allow me to move toward acceptance.

Sprawling over the bed, I stare at the wooden wall across the room. A familiar worry rekindles. Father. Is he really all right? Countless months have squeezed between us and pushed us farther apart every day. Just one minute with him ... just one minute to tell him I love him ...

I roll onto my stomach. Why am I worrying? The King of the universe holds my father in His hands. When will I stop itching to control and let God take over?

A golden finger of sunlight slips through the window and rests on me. I lift my head and stare out the window. Ribbons of red, pink, and orange swirl through the sky, stretching to the horizon. Glittering the waves, they twirl around a shining golden ball making its way home.

CHAPTER 10

A day later I squeeze through the sailors and run to the railing. Land bursting with color and life meets my gaze. Julinar. Beautiful Julinar. Sunlight streams onto the harbor just waves away from us. How long I have waited for this moment!

Captain Carrington appears at my side and extends his elbow. "Your Highness, allow me to escort you to the Julinarin estate."

I curl my arm through his, smiling up at him. Through our short time together, Captain Carrington has looked after me with a kindness that has touched me, and I'm now glad to call him a friend. "Thank you, Captain Carrington. I greatly appreciate it."

Making our way to the gangplank, I take in countless numbers of people, all cheering and waving. Some toss brightly colored flowers into our path; others smile through tears. A group of soldiers stand beside the gangplank. After meeting with them, they lead me to a carriage, and then we begin the ride to the mansion.

I lean against the carriage's seat, closing my eyes and letting the warm memories come flooding back. I can't wait to see Angelet.

Minutes later the carriage slows to a stop. I step out, and we walk to the entrance, where soldiers pull the huge doors open, revealing my home away from home.

"Lorelle?"

The clear, beautiful sound is all too familiar. I spin, and my gaze lands on Angelet, positioned like a queen high on the staircase.

She races down the steps, her hair and skirts flowing. I break away from the captain and let my feet carry me across the room as fast as they can go.

We fly into each other's arms, squealing, crying, and laughing like two little girls. We draw back, and Angelet's blue eyes sparkle and dance, her whole face aglow with tears.

"Oh, Lorelle!" she exclaims, holding my face. "Thank God you're all right." She steps back and examines me. "Oh, look at you—dirty, and your dress tattered and soiled." Her voice lowers, and sorrow mars her pretty face. "And these scars—what on earth have they done to you?"

I shake my head as we walk up the stairs.

"I've been sick with worry," she continues. "Just sick. We couldn't find you, and then the king sent word you were being held for ransom. I felt I would die." Once we are out of earshot of the others, she pauses and clasps my hands. "Really, Lorelle, how are you?"

I blink and pull her hands closer to me. "Oh, Angelet," I whisper, "it was horrible. Every day I wondered if I would ever get out of that place, and every day nothing happened."

She rubs her fingers over the tops of my hands. "God never stopped protecting you, I know. And He answered my prayer. He brought you back safely."

I feel a smile surface on my face. I want to tell her everything I've learned about Him, but I detect the all-too-familiar grin creeping onto her face. Suddenly we're both laughing again, our hands squeezing tighter. We turn and continue walking up the steps. I didn't realize before how much she means to me and how much she reminds me of my mother.

"Now," Angelet starts, "you need a hot bath before we present you to Lord Harmon. And a new dress! Good heavens, child, the one you're in now is in absolute ruins."

I laugh as I take in the holes, tears, and smudges covering my gown. The color has faded, and any adornments have completely fallen off. I haven't seen my reflection in a month—no doubt I look quite different from the girl who was running through the woods not so long ago.

When we reach my bedchamber, a servant opens the door. I slip inside. My clothes and personal belongings still camp in my open wardrobe and on my nightstand. Everything is the exact way I left it.

Angelet crosses the room to the wardrobe and brings out a silky blue gown. After a glance at me, she makes her way to the water closet. Ringing the bell beside the door, she then opens it and waits for me to enter.

Inside, I stare at my image in the mirror. The girl staring back has thin skin stretched over her face, her lips cracked and pale. My nails are chipped and broken. A large scar zigzags across the upper right side of my head. Other smaller scars surface here and there, black and blue bruises hide in corners, and a ratty, tangled nest of hair sits above it all.

At first I'm horrified. Yet the way my hair twists perfectly to look like a rat's nest ... I look absolutely ridiculous. "Oh, good heavens! I had no idea ..."

Angelet laughs. "You definitely don't look like you did when I last saw you. The dirt is of course completely washable. But, my dear—what awful scars! And the large one. Whatever happened?"

"They knocked me out when I fought back, when they first captured me." My stomach writhes again into that knot. Sir Wellington. And Angelet ... why is she avoiding his death with me?

I force my mind back to my train of thought, to anything but him. "I was cared for during my stay there. Two dear servants treated me like a queen." I smile as I think of the couple back in Alandar. Maybe someday ...

My thoughts splash apart as a maid appears at the door.

"Anne, please prepare a bath for Princess Lorelle," Angelet orders.

The maid nods and leaves.

"Leave the dress here, and let us go back to your bedchamber," Angelet says. She links her arm in mine and leads us to my room.

Once inside, she sets her fingers to unlacing my dress. "Lord Harmon and your father have been discussing your predicament for quite some time. King Maurice demanded a large sum of money, plus land in Julinar. His first request was ridiculous. Your father bargained with him for a while and finally reached a manageable sum. The money was taken out of the Julinarin treasury here at the estate, and Lord Harmon wrote the land deeds and then gave them and the money to Captain Carrington."

I press my lips together. My capture has cost my father much. Even the people of Julinar have paid for my release.

I meet her gaze in the mirror, breathe in, and give her an account of my capture in full, pulling out every moment and detail.

Once I finish, she moves her hands to my upper arms and rests her chin on my shoulder. "God never fails."

I can only nod.

She squeezes my shoulders. "You have grown more in these last weeks than in all your seventeen years. God never left your side."

"Excuse me, me lady," a quiet voice breaks in, "but the princess's bath is ready."

"Thank you, Anne." Angelet rolls my old dress into a ball and hands it to the maid. "We shall be right in." She turns back to me. "Come now. Time for you to have a good, solid wash." A grin spreads across her face.

I need no persuading.

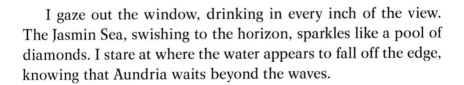

I gaze out the window, drinking in every inch of the view. The Jasmin Sea, swishing to the horizon, sparkles like a pool of diamonds. I stare at where the water appears to fall off the edge, knowing that Aundria waits beyond the waves.

I smile as I think of Angelet's joy-filled response to my redemption. She didn't wait a moment to give me a Bible of my own, a treasure to lead and guide me all my life. Each word I've read has seemed to come alive, jumping from the pages into my heart.

I turn and lock my gaze on my door. What else lies beyond it? Besides a few selected rooms here and there, I really haven't seen much of the mansion ...

I slip into the hall, making my way to the marble staircase. Two steps down, I hear a noise rising from the foyer and stop. What is that?

I shake off the sound and continue down, yet my eyes stray to the direction of the noise. Below me, a door opens and shuts. A group of men emerge and wind their way toward the staircase. I grab the railing.

The one in front—blond hair and incredibly blue eyes ...

I fly down the staircase. My heart climbs to my throat, threatening to break through my body. Sir Wellington ... James ... alive ...

He catches sight of me and lowers himself into a deep bow as I halt in front of him. "Your Highness."

My cheeks flush with what feels like fire. Why did I run down the staircase?

I lift my chin. "It is good to see you well and healthy."

"Thank you, Your Highness," he answers, grinning. "And if I may say, I am relieved to see you here safe and secure."

I twist my fingers as I try to steady my rapid breathing. How on earth did he ...?

"Did you return safely to the castle ... that day?" My tongue sticks to the roof of my mouth.

He laughs under his breath. "I was out hunting with a friend, but we had split up for a little while. Hours later he came back and found me on the beach."

"How does your injury fare?" My heart won't slow down. How was he not killed? All those weeks thinking he was dead ...

"It is healing slowly," he answers. "It has only been the past week I have been able to be on my feet."

Though I long to throw my arms around him in relief, I straighten my shoulders and smile. "Well, Sir Wellington, I am relieved to find you alive."

He returns the smile. "Thank you. I feel the same for you. You had me very concerned."

His eyes scour my face, and any form of confidence shrivels as I realize he is taking in my hideous bruises and scars. But why do I care?

I push a curl behind my ear. "Sir Wellington, thank you for what you did that day. You risked your life."

"I would gladly do it again." A spark flashes in his serious eyes. "If you'll excuse me, Your Highness, I must be going. It was an honor seeing you again."

He bows as I nod, and then follows after the group of men. I stare after him, the shock chilling my spine.

I slowly turn and walk through the mansion, my mind replaying and replaying the short exchange and again visualizing the spark in his eyes.

I stop short and turn my head. Men's voices drift through a meeting room door next to where I stand.

"They're gaining power, especially now that they have part of this small country," a deep voice rumbles.

"Their attempt to take over Aundria before Julinar never really panned out, though Alandarin forces are still planted in the country," a different voice breaks in. "I have a feeling they will now come to us."

I lean forward and press closer to the door.

"Do you think they'll make an attempt to capture the princess again?"

An eerie silence pinches the air.

"Perhaps," someone finally answers. "Alandar is unpredictable. They had great success in holding her for ransom. We must keep her safe and closely guarded."

I gulp and back away from the door, wishing I hadn't heard.

Turning, I continue down the hallway and walk back up the staircase. I pull open a door I've never noticed before. A long flight of stairs leading to one of the mansion's many towers extends past the doorway. The walls lining the tower's staircase practically touch each of my shoulders as I climb. At the top, a round room meets my gaze. Chests line most of the room, and tall, silver candlestands weave throughout them. Draped cloth hangs from the ceiling, and two bows and quivers filled with arrows position themselves against a wall. A large window pours in light.

A thin layer of dust covers everything. I sigh as I imagine having a place like this to be alone and undisturbed …

I cross to the window and lean out. Mountains piled upon mountains reach for the heavens. A sheet of pure blue sky stretches above the miles of island.

Despite the beauty outside my window, my thoughts crawl back to Alandar and their next move. If they come to Julinar, what exactly will they do?

The Julinarin treasury lies in one of the mansion's towers. Would Alandar try to seal their fingers around that? Lord Harmon has told me which tower it lies hidden in, one not so far away from the one I'm in now. How safe is it?

I look back to the horizon. Just beyond lies Aundria and my father, the man I love more than anyone or anything in the world. I bite my lip and send up a silent prayer for him, for the man who has loved me unconditionally, for the man who has never left my side. Until now.

———◀◦▶———

I flip open the covers of my bed and lift my knee onto the mattress. Before I crawl in, my eyes wander to the night sky. Stars twinkle through my window as the moon duplicates itself on the Jasmin water. With a clear night like this, what would the view from the tower room I just discovered look like?

I turn and throw my pelisse over my shoulders and then slip out of the bedchamber. The mansion glows from candles seated

79

in sconces on the walls. Looking past the guards, I see no one. My heels hardly touch the floor as I head for the tower door, gathering part of my pelisse at the neck. Quietly, I slip through the door and hurry up the staircase. Soft, twinkling light flits down, and already the sweet air of the courtyard outside wraps around me. Quickening my pace, I reach the top, but before I enter, I stop short.

Sir Wellington stands at the window, hands on the sill, gazing into the starry night. He turns his head. "Your Highness!"

Is that delight in his tone? I shift my feet, turning to go. "I beg your pardon, Sir Wellington."

He steps forward, his hand outstretched to stop me. "No, no, don't go. I came only to admire the view. Why have you come?"

I tilt my chin. "The view."

He grins, his blue eyes sparkling. "Well, do come and join me then."

Intertwining my fingers, I make my way over to him. Reaching the window, the night breeze spreads through my hair and cools my neck like a whisper.

Against a pure, deep-blue blanket, the stars sparkle like diamonds. The moon shines over the rippling water, flooding the waves with a white glow. The lights of Camwind gleam like gold stars.

The sight leaves me breathless. "It's beautiful."

"It is. I like to come here to breathe and relax. A sight like this is truly calming."

I nod and stare toward the mountains that stand like dark shadows in the night.

Silence settles down. I smile, awed by the incredible beauty before me.

Daring a peek at him, I tighten my hands around the windowsill. "Sir Wellington," I begin, "I was quite relieved to find you alive. For weeks I thought you were dead."

"It was also a true relief to me to find you here unharmed," he replies. "I never stopped thinking about you and wondering how they were treating you there."

80

"I was all right." I pause and tilt my head toward him. "I've thought a great deal about what you told me that day, a month back."

"Yes." Not a hint of confusion touches his voice.

"Well, I discovered for myself what you said." I steal a glance at his face then stare back into the night. "I wanted to thank you. If it weren't for the message you shared with me that day, I don't think I would have survived my stay in Alandar—or be able to survive every day that stands before me."

Out of the corner of my eye, I see him smile. "It wasn't me, Your Highness."

My face breaks into a grin, the wave of excitement I experienced during that night in the dungeon washing over me again. Gratitude for my maker follows in its wake. I know the man beside me shares the exact same feeling.

"Did they hurt you much while you were there?" he suddenly asks.

I turn to him. "Well, nothing that won't heal, I guess."

He faces me and gently brushes a finger over a bruise on my forehead. "I hate that you were there."

I cock my head. "Well, I'm back now, aren't I?"

He fingers one of my curls. "I'm sorry I couldn't stop them."

"No, no. Don't do that to yourself."

He shakes his head. "If I would have just parried that blow, you would have been safe."

"You got stabbed in the side!"

"And you were locked in that tyrant's dungeon."

A sliver of night breeze slips through the window and cools the air between us. "Yet that was where God decided to rescue me."

He stops fingering my hair. "And He brought you back to me."

A cloud slides over the moon, stealing some of the tower's light. Neither of us says anything. Our breathing is the only sound.

I spin and grasp the railing, clasping so tightly my fingers burn. "I'm sorry about your side. I guess you have me to blame for that."

He chuckles and sets his hands on the railing, next to mine. "I would go through it again to keep you safe."

My lips curve in a smile as his words settle in the air. Looking up, I see a small shooting star, far off in the distance, spring through the sky.

He quietly reaches his hand over and places it on top of mine. "It is amazing, isn't it?"

This time I know he doesn't mean the view.

CHAPTER 11

The alarm pierces the night's quiet. I jump from my bed and race to the window. Stopping in the moonlight, I grab the window's side. Alandarin soldiers stream from their ships to the docks. Soldiers rain on the village and the castle.

I charge from the window out of my room, scrambling to a halt in the hall. Not one person meets my eyes. Are the soldiers on their way now? Which way to go?

"Princess Lorelle!"

I spin around. Sir Wellington rushes over to me. Grabbing my hand, he begins pulling me. "Come with me. Now!"

"No, wait!" I tear my hand from his clutch.

"No, we have absolutely no time to lose. We can't let them capture you again!"

He grasps my hand and jerks me toward him as he begins to run. I follow, stumbling.

"They've forced a surprise attack on us, haven't they?" I ask.

"Yes," he pants. "We've got to get you to safety."

We run down a stone staircase enveloped in dark. Hallways with wet, dark bricks rush past us. I risk a peek at his anxious face. Right then, he is an exact image of his father, playing the same role his father played the night of my escape from Aundria.

The ground softens. Dirt. How far down are we going? My chest tightens with fatigue. When will we reach Sir Wellington's intended destination?

We run down another flight of steps. Then down another hall. Black shadows and eerie light mingle through the air as we brush past dark walls.

I ram into Sir Wellington's shoulders. He slaps his hands on the dirt wall next to us. I bend down and brace my hands against my knees, trying to catch my breath.

Something clicks. Looking up, I watch the knight pull open a hidden door. "In—now."

I stiffen. Looking into the dark hole, empty and so far underground, I suddenly know. I know I can't just sit, keeping only myself safe, as others fight for our country with their lives.

Sir Wellington grabs my shoulders and thrusts me into the opening.

"Stay here." His voice mirrors the dark shadows on the walls.

I catch his arm as he turns to leave. "Where do you think you're going?"

"I'll be back."

"I can't just stay here. Let me—"

"You'll be safest here."

I step in front of him and lock eyes with him. "You've seen me shoot, Sir Wellington. Give me a bow and quiver and a position high in a tower."

"You're mad," he returns, shuffling his feet.

"No, I'm not. The Alandarins won't be able to see me, and I know what I can do."

He shifts his weight from one foot to the other, uneasy. "We can't risk that. You don't know what they'll do to you if they get hold of you a second time." He brushes past me.

"Sir Wellington, please!" My face tightens. How can I just sit and wait while everyone else struggles above me?

He keeps his broad back to me. "No."

I lift my chin. This isn't just a knight carrying out orders. This isn't even just protection. What else is beneath his actions?

He finally turns to me, his blue eyes so bright with suffering I'm caught off guard. He fumbles for a minute, lines of pain and regret etched across his face. He drops his gaze.

"Sir Wellington?"

His words fall out in a whisper. "Please ... just stay safe ... Lorelle."

And he takes off running.

I stand glued to the ground, heart pounding. The sound of my name on his lips fills my head like a beautiful melody. Eerie moonlight blurs with the dark as I replay his words in my head. I slide a hand over my chest and lean against the wall, staring after where he disappeared. Faint shouts and clashes sound somewhere in the distance.

The cold air pushes against me as I take off running down the hallway. I run up the steps I just ran down, turn down winding hallways, and stop.

Two sets of dirt stairways stand before me. My tongue scrapes across my mouth like dry sand. The mansion's underground tunnels could lead anywhere. Where am I to go now?

Dirt lies shuffled on the first set of steps. The other holds its dirt packed hard and tight. I sprint up the first set of steps. Once at the top, I run through another hallway, recognizing markings and following them. Hallway after hallway, staircase after staircase ... my feet weigh me down like bricks. Needles of pain jerk through my sides.

Relief washes through me as I reach the staircase leading to the floor of my bedchamber. I dart up the steps and run to the tower door then stop.

I'm completely alone. A gold light comes from the windows, and by the shadows dancing against the stars, I realize with horror it's fire. Every muffled shriek, every muffled yell, every muffled clash throws chills down my back. I turn and pull the tower door open, shut it behind me, then dash up the steps into the little room.

Everything is quiet. Only last night a knight and I stood there, unaware of what was coming.

I grab one of the quivers full of arrows and sling it over my shoulder. Grasping a bow, I rush to the window and halt.

Alandarin and Julinarin soldiers cut and slash at each other in the mansion's front yard. Soldiers soaked in blood lie scattered over the ground, some grabbing the soil as if to breathe. Shrieks and yells freeze my blood.

I gulp and reach back, grip an arrow, and position it in the bow. I focus on my first target and draw in a long breath. *King Jesus, please help me.*

I release the arrow. It shoots through the air and hits an Alandarin soldier.

I reach back for another arrow and send it flying. Another Alandarin drops to the ground. Two more shrink as arrows dig into their chests.

Soldiers turn their gazes toward my tower, but then are distracted as more Aundrian arrows rain down from nearby towers. I step deeper into the shadows and draw another arrow.

A knot bullies my shoulder as I continue reaching back. My fingers burn as they become raw beneath the bowstring.

Back, release, back, release … I release another and throw my hand back for another. I snatch only air. I fling the quiver off my back and swing the second in its place. As I charge another arrow into the bow, a verse I read earlier today floods back to me: "I can do all things through Christ who strengthens me."

Doors slam. Pounding feet and muffled voices erupt below. Soldiers. They're near my bedchamber.

I shake my shoulders and continue shooting, quickening my speed. Soreness grips my arm like a claw.

A shock rumbles through the castle and sends me ramming into the wall. I collapse to my knees, my bow jagging into my side. What hit the castle? Pulling out my bow from underneath me, I listen, motionless against the wall. Nothing. I'm still alone.

I pull myself to my feet and position myself again in front of the window. As I place another arrow and draw back the bowstring, the floors shake again. I grab the window's side, dropping the bow. The castle rocks beneath my feet like an earthquake. Seconds pass before the floors finally calm. I push myself from the window and pick up my fallen bow.

Feet thump on the tower stairs. Soldiers. I throw my hand back and seize an arrow, aiming it toward the stairway. Three Alandarins trample up the staircase. I release the arrow. One crumples into a heap. I grab another arrow when a second lunges for me. I drop the bow and plunge the arrow into his flesh with my hand. When he collapses, I shoot my eyes at the third and stop still.

His glistening sword is inches from my chin. He grins at me, his eyes gleaming. "All right, little missy, the treasury. Which tower is it in?"

I'm silent, staring into his eyes.

He touches my chin with the tip of his sword. "C'mon, now." His giant figure looms over me, his dark eyes and shining armor piercing me.

"Fine then!" he yells. He reaches for my neck.

I grab his wrist as he clasps my neck and raises his sword. He shoves me against the wall and lifts his sword higher. I've barely choked out a scream when the castle lurches.

Crashes and shrieks deafen me as I'm hurled to the floor. The tower roof caves in. Stones crash down, folding over and swallowing everything like the sea. I throw my arms over my head.

Dark suffocates me. I bury my head deeper into my arms and clench my body as everything crashes around me.

Silence. The wind rustles through the trees. My ears buzz. I lie still, gulping in air. Under a blanket of small stones, my legs feel frozen, like they're trapped in huge blocks of ice. Gray dust encloses me, filtering into my lungs. Slowly, I brush the stones away but stop short. A million jagged rocks seem to be piercing my legs.

The pain is so intense I cry out, sweat drenching my forehead and chest. I dig my nails into my hands, my whole body shaking.

The soldier. I spin my head around to look for him. Silver glistens through a heap of stones. Blood trickles through the pile into a large puddle.

I wince and tear my gaze away. An icy sensation shivers up my spine. I draw in a deep breath, close my eyes, and pull my upper body up by my arms. Once upright, the pain in my legs shoots to my stomach. My teeth grind into my lip as I lift my head.

A tower wall collapsed with the roof. The rest still stands, their tops jagged and uneven. The sky stretches above me like a black hand, ready to pounce on me any minute. Tonight no stars appear. Dark and eeriness swirls through the air like black mud.

I need to get out of here. But where would I go? And who could help me? Maybe I just need to sit here and wait for the battle to end, but what if it doesn't end in the way I hope? What if Alandar defeats Julinar? Or what if I'm never found? Any movement only sharpens the pain in my legs. And what if, while I lie here, more soldiers come? I shiver, thinking about the three lifeless bodies around me. What if more of the castle collapses? What if …?

Soft realization trickles into me. He is here. Even while I lie helpless and suffering, God is here. I gulp, tears of pain beginning to run down my cheeks. *Oh, God, please help me! Please. I don't know what to do. I'm scared!* A wave of calm and warmth covers me. Through my throat, to my chest, my hands, my fingertips, He pours out His strength and peace. I close my eyes and breathe. He's here. Everything is all right. Everything is all right.

God is here … God is here … God is here …

I lay my head back and close my eyes.

CHAPTER 12

My eyelids flutter open. Light dazzles me. I squint and move my head. When it feels like the light softens, I open my eyes wider.

Angelet sits at the foot of a bed I'm lying in. Two maids stand by a doorway. I scan the room. My bedchamber.

Angelet glances at me. "Lorelle!" Relief lights her face as she slides closer to me. "How do you feel?"

I stop for a minute. "Fine." Is that cracked, husky voice mine? "What … what happened?"

"You broke your leg and sprained your other ankle. The physician said you'll just need to rest and let them heal."

A quiet knock taps on the door. Angelet turns and answers, "Come."

Lord Harmon steps into the room. Instantly his eyes land on me. A smile shines on his face that is wrinkled with fatigue. "Princess Lorelle, I am glad to see you awake." He steps into the room. "How are you feeling?"

I give him the same answer. "Fine."

"I was quite alarmed when a soldier came to me with you in his arms, unconscious and bloody," he tells me, tugging at his vest. "He told me he found you in a tower under a heap of stones."

"But—the battle?"

He runs a hand through his hair. "We succeeded in pushing the Alandarin army away from the estate and Camwind, but they have various camps planted throughout the island. We have soldiers working to keep them away from here and force them out, but so far, we've succeeded in only the former."

I wriggle my arm beneath the cover. "How many were killed?"

A shadow covers his face. "Many. We also had quite a few valuable lords, knights, and soldiers captured."

"Was Sir Wellington among them?" The question slips out before I can stop it.

Lord Harmon rubs his jaw. "He was."

I crumple the sheets in my hand. My chest tautens as shock springs through my body. "When did you discover his absence?"

"Only after the Alandarins left was it obvious who was missing." A grave veil darkens his face as he tucks his thumbs in his belt. "It took us hours to find you in the shattered tower. Parts of the mansion were destroyed. They used a battering ram in various places."

I try to move further up my pillow. "They didn't get the treasury, did they?"

"Thank goodness, no," he answers. "Now please excuse me, Your Highness, but I ordered Sir Wellington to take you to an underground room for safety. Whatever were you doing in that tower?"

———◆◇◆———

Angelet slips into my bedroom, her blue eyes sparkling. "The Aundrian ship will be leaving tomorrow. I'm sure you heard all the commotion in the village."

I nod, remembering the ship's arrival yesterday. As I shift my weight from my almost-healed leg to the other, she crosses to me and extends her hand. "A letter for you." A grin spreads across her face. "It's from your father."

Instant longing for him comes rushing back. I grab the letter from her, tear it open, and begin reading.

After I finish, I look out the window. Angelet's quiet voice breaks into my thoughts.

"My, your face is a sight to behold. What did your father say, if I may ask?"

I rub the fabric of my dress between my fingers. "Oh, he just informed me about Aundria's condition and such. They have completely pushed the Alandarin forces out." I let a little smile surface. "Their strength and perseverance pulled them through. He said he misses me and is doing the best he can to push through without my mother and me by his side." Biting my lip, I fold the letter. "He and my mother were inseparable. They never made a decision without the other's advice." The glass of the window cools my fingertips as I brush them over the surface. "He hopes I will be able to come home soon, but for safety reasons, he wants me to stay here a little longer. Nothing is certain there yet."

She walks to the window and runs her hands along the sill. "I understand. Hopefully it will not be too long until you can return."

I nod, staring at the sea's waves. She rubs my shoulder and leaves me alone.

My cheek tickles beneath the cold of the glass as I lean my face on the window. I want so badly to go home and to see my father. I would do anything to feel his arms around me, keeping me safe. And Sir Wellington. I want him out of prison more than I can bear. What have they been doing to him the past four weeks he's been there? And every other Julinarin who was captured the night of the attack?

———◄○►———

Flickering candle shadows dance in my room. I turn on my pillow and stare into the inky night. Faint silhouettes of clouds slide through the sky.

A knock sounds on the door. I know who it will be. The door slides open, and a second later Angelet slips inside. She crosses to the bed and sits down beside me. "How are you doing?"

"I'm all right." I bunch up my pillow and sink my head into it, hiding part of my view.

91

"Well, I wanted to see how you're doing and bid you good night." She rubs her hands slowly over her face and releases a long breath. "Sweet dreams, my dear."

I roll to my other side. "Are you all right?"

She cocks her head toward me and gives me a small smile. "I'm fine, my dear. Thank you."

Those eyes tell me otherwise. I prop myself up on my elbow. "There is something, isn't there?"

This time a heavy sigh slips from her lips as she massages the back of her neck. "We received a message from King Maurice today."

I sit all the way up and lean forward, the back of my neck suddenly hot. "What did it say?"

She rubs her hands together. "He's executed our captured soldiers and is holding our knights and lords for ransom." Her gaze shifts to the wall. "The money and land he wants is unbelievably expensive. We can't spare what he is demanding. However, if we don't give him what he wants, he'll execute all his prisoners."

I stare at her and grip the blanket with my hand, clutching so tightly my hand cramps.

"And we know he won't stop there," she continues. "He'll wage another attack on us, for certain. With how we're struggling already, we won't be able to win." She stops for a minute, lost in thought. "We did convince him, though, to give us some time. We're hoping to get as much help as we can from Aundria. Plans will be formed and carried out."

I know exactly what she means. Every second counts now. Julinar stands on the brink.

"Do you think if we come together again we can defeat Alandar?"

She pulls at one of her curls. "Aundria is gaining strength every day. We do think that possibly, together, we might be able to beat them, but that's a big might."

"None of us expected them to come here, did we?"

She shakes her head. "Not at first, no. That's why you were sent here." Another sigh slips from her mouth. "We were wrong."

I turn from her and stare into the night. Only months ago I was in Aundria, safe with two parents who loved me. What happened?

"Well, get some rest. I'll see you in the morning," she says.

The hope in her blue eyes is enough to encourage me. "Thank you, Angelet." As she rises from the bed to leave, one last question, dry as sand and cold as ice, crawls off my tongue. "How much time do we have?"

She pauses with her hand on the knob and looks at me. "Four weeks."

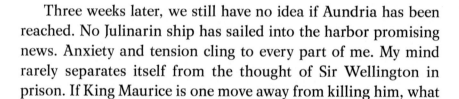

Three weeks later, we still have no idea if Aundria has been reached. No Julinarin ship has sailed into the harbor promising news. Anxiety and tension cling to every part of me. My mind rarely separates itself from the thought of Sir Wellington in prison. If King Maurice is one move away from killing him, what is his treatment toward the knight like now?

A knock sounds on my door, and I give the consent to enter. Angelet's eyes dance as she enters. "Look out your window."

I stand from my vanity table and cross to the window. The waves of the sea roll against each other again and again, and I follow them with my eyes to the horizon.

"A ship!"

"Yes, a ship." She stands beside me, her gaze fixed on the tiny dot miles away.

"It has to be one of ours," I say, wanting more than stating.

She grins. "That's what we're hoping."

I pull back the curtain further then ruffle its edges. Turning to the bookcase, I straighten some stray volumes and wipe away some dust. It floats through the air and dissipates in the study's carpet.

If only the time to wait for the ship would disappear that quickly.

Lord Harmon bursts into the room, leaving the door swinging on its hinges. I stare at him in surprise, my hand still on the bookcase.

"Lord Harmon."

He hurries a bow. "Your Highness." He quickly straightens and takes a step closer to me. "An Alandarin ship has just pulled into our harbor."

I drop a hand on the chair next to me. Not an Aundrian ship? For a moment I stare at the floor, trying to shove the news into acceptance. "Thank you for telling me."

"I will be going to meet the ship," he continues. "I want you to stay in your bedchamber until they leave—with the door locked."

I nod and walk over to him. "I will be waiting."

He kisses my hand. "Thank you, Princess. Until then."

He turns and leaves the room, his firm footsteps echoing across the floor. Walking to the entrance, I stop and stare at the winding main staircase crawling to the ceiling far above.

Alandarins. The word burns in my throat.

My footsteps throw an eerie, lonely sound into the air. I scrape my tongue across my mouth as I arrive at the top of the stairs and walk into my bedroom. Why are they here?

———◄○►———

Staring out my window, I watch the Alandarin lords, knights, and soldiers leave the estate. My fingers twist together.

I turn and rush out of my room. After making my way downstairs, I run to the meeting room where I hear Lord Harmon's voice mingle with others. I stop at the door and knock.

After a moment, it swings open, and Lord Barkinten stands before me. He bows with cordiality. "Your Highness, do come in."

I thank him and enter the room. Lord Harmon sits at the head of a long table lined with lords. He looks up at me, his mouth set in a harsh line. Rising to his feet, he lowers himself in a bow.

I walk to the table. "What did the Alandarin lords want?"

He widens his fingers on the table. He knows I've been wanting to ask the question for some time.

He lifts his chin. "They came to collect the money and land deeds King Maurice is demanding." The words crawl through his tight lips.

A week early? I try to read his eyes. The sum is no doubt large. With no financial help from Aundria, how can we afford it?

"They are now spending the night in Camwind," he continues, running his hands over the wood of the table. His gaze corners mine. "You know as well as I do that we don't have the money here at the Julinarin estate. And we still have not heard from Aundria."

I rub my hand up my arm. "Are you going to give them more land in place of money?"

"The island isn't that big."

My shoulders twitch as I draw in a breath. I stare at him. "Then what are you going to do?"

"We're discussing possibilities. God give us grace."

By the look on his face, I know he wants to end the discussion there. I nod and curtsy. "Thank you, Lord Harmon. I will retire now."

He bows and gives me one last glance, this one still sharp but carrying slight gentleness. We both know.

I turn and leave the room. Once the door shuts behind me, I stop and press my face into my hands. Dread hardens into a rock inside me.

We will lose. And the captives in Alandar will die.

There's no other choice. Unless by some miracle an Aundrian ship pulls into port tomorrow.

I turn and run up the staircase into my bedroom. Flopping on the bed, I curl into a ball, arms around my middle, trying to shove my stomach back down from my throat. Burying my face in my bed, my mind twists and fights so hard I feel ripped to shreds.

I pull myself off the bed and walk to my window. The Alandarin ship drifts on the water, silhouetted against the evening sky like a black hawk. Maybe King Maurice will use the Julinarin prisoners for slaves and spare their lives … yet I know that won't happen. King Maurice will delight in slaughtering all of them. There are enough slaves in Alandar and not a speck of mercy in the king's soul. Any chance of survival shrinks to almost nothing.

I spin around from the window. What if—? Could I—?

I rush to my wardrobe and fling open the doors. Grasping my dark-blue cloak that will cover my entire body, I throw it on the bed and grab two leather bags. I cross over to the table beside my bed, clasp my Bible, and carefully place it in one of the bags. I run my hands through a drawer in my wardrobe and pull out paper, a small sealed bottle of ink, and a quill. I then reach into a smaller drawer and grab a large handful of Aundria penses, enough for the cost I need, and place them in the bag with the Bible.

Kneeling down, I press the paper against my legs. The ink drips onto my dress as I bring the quill to my paper and begin to write. My hand cramps as the minutes go by. A crow calls outside my window. When I'm finished, I roll up the paper and hide it in the bag with my Bible. Placing that to my side, I then open a drawer at the bottom of the wardrobe and pull out a pair of brown breeches and a short white tunic, the clothes I bribed away from a servant years ago and used over and over to wear when sneaking out of the castle to climb trees. I run my hands along the worn, rough fabric, grateful that my mother unknowingly grabbed them when she gathered the rest of my clothes the night of the attack. Pressing them to my nose, I inhale deeply. The sweet scent of pine needles with a hint of sap fills my nostrils.

Twisting my arms around my back to undo my dress, I peel it off my body and toss it on the bed. I pull the breeches on, throw the tunic over my shoulders, and then tuck it in.

Before I ring the bell for a maid, I rack my brain for a servant who will be best suited to help me. Eldon, one of the stablehands, comes to mind. I've seen him working and have noticed his strength and diligence. He will do.

Finally I ring the bell. A minute later soft footsteps sound on the stairs, followed by a tapping on my door. I pull it open, hiding all my body but my head.

"Please inform Eldon I wish to speak him."

"Yes, Your Highness. I will tell him to wait for you at the foot of the stairs, if that pleases you."

"Thank you, Anne."

I shut the door behind her and turn back to my room. I throw my cloak over my shoulders within seconds. I bend down, blow out the candle, and grab the bags.

I peek out of the doorway. Only guards are in sight, so I slip out of the room, silently shutting the door behind me, and tiptoe down the long staircase.

Eldon gives a quick bow when I reach the bottom.

"Eldon," I begin.

"Your Highness?"

"Uh, may you ..." I stop. "Follow me."

"Certainly, Your Highness." His eyes run over me, taking in my cloak and bags.

I turn and hurry down the back hallway, until I come to the kitchen at the back of mansion. I push open the door and creep inside, Eldon right behind me.

He shoots me a look. Darkness engulfs every corner of the room except for moonlight filtering in from a barred window in the wall. I take in his square broad shoulders, thick arms, tall height. His eyes hold my gaze sharply but calmly, evenly but carefully, waiting with expectation.

I made the right choice.

"Eldon," I begin again, "I need you to accompany me ... on a journey."

His eyebrows rise slightly.

"It will be dangerous. I cannot guarantee your safety. Do you understand?"

He slowly nods.

I open my mouth to say more but stop. Silence pounds the air. My words will carry. Too far.

"Come with me."

I walk to one of the counters and fill the second leather bag with bread, cheese, apples, and oranges. Noticing a row of pegs holding up a handful of cloaks, I grab one and throw it to Eldon. As he sweeps it over his shoulders, I pull my own cloak's hood far over my face. I then grab a rope on top of a barrel and sling the two bags through it. Tying it around my waist, I hide them amid the folds of my cloak.

"Stay at my side."

The door creaks open as I steal out of the room, Eldon next to me. I run again down the dark hallway, not stopping until I reach the door I slipped out of the day I was captured.

"Let us pass," I command the guards posted there, my voice loud enough for only them to hear.

They obey and swing the huge slabs open with slow groans. I wince, wondering if anyone has heard. Fresh breeze sweeps in, chilling me. The sun has set, adding darkness to my cover. I nod to the guards, motion to Eldon with my head, and slip out.

Outside, everything holds an eerie silence except for the rustling of leaves.

Eldon's expression speaks everything running through his mind. He'll think I'm mad. Perhaps I am.

Breaking into a slow run, I head for the back gate used only for the servants. Selected soldiers line the fence.

I lean toward Eldon's ear. "We are simply two servants buying supplies for the dinner tomorrow night. You are to tell them while I stand behind you. Understand?"

He nods, despite the suspicion glinting in his eyes, and we hurry to the gate.

"Two servants ordered to buy supplies in the village for the dinner tomorrow night." Eldon's voice rings firm. I keep my head low, standing behind his wide shoulders.

The soldiers nod, familiar with the routine, and unlock the iron doors and pull them open. Am I really about to do this?

Eldon thanks the soldiers and walks through the entrance, my steps right behind his. The heavy doors clang shut behind me.

We walk the path to Camwind, where golden lights streaming from windows light the streets. I pull my hood lower over my face, my chin almost touching my chest. As we near the port, we ease into hiding behind trees, carts, and barrels and silently steal our way to the water. Waves lap onto the shore. When we reach the Alandarin ship, I lift my head to the mast then glance at the soldiers standing guard beside it. They stand like statues, frozen in the wind.

My eyes scan the ship again. Netting hangs over the ship's side down to the water. Small round windows line the side around it. I grin.

I open one of the leather bags and bring out the note, sticking it in the upper part of my braid. Nodding to Eldon, I emerge from behind a stack of crates and silently wade into the water. None of the soldiers turn.

As the sand leaves our toes, we break into as quiet of a swim as we can. My breaths fall out in gasps as the sharp chill of the water seeps through my clothes.

When I reach the netting, I grab the mesh and pull myself up, climbing it like a rope. The wind catches hold of it and swings it to the side.

My foot slips free. I lose my balance as my hand slides down. My leg ramming into the ship's side, I desperately flail and grab the net. I freeze. My heart chokes my throat. Instant fear of whether the soldiers heard and will turn and see grips me. I look down at Eldon. He is pasted to the side of the ship, eyes on me, signaling me not to move or make a sound. I slide my eyes to the side where the soldiers are.

Nothing.

My breath rushes out in relief. Tightening my grip, I climb higher until I reach the railing above. I clench it with my hands, sweep my leg over the wood, and slide onto the ship.

Silence freezes the air. I crouch beside the railing, sucking in air as relief squeezes through my limbs. A new sound crawls into my ears. I crouch lower and listen, straining my ears. A second later I smile. Snoring.

As I feel my head to make sure the note is still secure in the upper part of my braid, I search the deck. A trapdoor lies in the floor in front of me.

Leaning my head back over the side, I look down at Eldon. "Climb up," I mouth.

For a moment he hesitates, looking at me, and then finally grabs the net and crawls up. Once he is over the side, I motion my head toward the trapdoor. He nods and moves across the deck, slowly opens it, and looks down. Then he gestures to me with a move of his head.

I creep over to him and peek down the hole. A ladder extends into complete darkness. He turns and climbs down it, his movements silent in the air, until he disappears into the black.

I ease onto the bars, carefully shutting the door over me. Nerves twist my stomach. Who else could be hiding in the shadows?

When I reach the bottom, I stretch my arms out in front of me and grope around, not daring to make a sound to Eldon. Only air slides between my fingers.

A hand presses against my mouth. I fling my hand to my face when breath slips into my ear. I can barely hear the word: "Quiet." It's Eldon.

Breathing out, I nod. Faint moonlight from the trapdoor's crisscrossed holes settle in the air, and a slightly open door to my side comes into view. Piles of crates, boxes, and barrels peek from behind it. Eldon sees it the same moment I do and nudges me forward.

We slip inside. Behind me, Eldon's footsteps lightly scrape the floor, and the door eases shut behind him.

Moonlight squeezes in from a window in the far wall, open and swinging in the breeze. Stopping next to a crate, I sink down, free to breathe. Eldon kneels next to me.

"You may be the destined queen, and I may be your servant," he whispers, "but if I may, I would like to ask what you're doing bringing me aboard an enemy ship—and what *you* are doing climbing aboard an enemy ship?"

I tilt my head. "I need you to deliver a message for me."

"I'm boarding an enemy ship to deliver a message?"

"In Alandar."

His eyes narrow.

I pause. "Please, I need you. Please—trust me."

His eyes study mine, his jaw tightening. He opens his mouth again, but I stop him with a hand to his arm. "Please, Eldon."

His eyes hold mine for a minute, silence between us, until he finally says, "Very well, Princess. I will do as you wish."

I breathe out. "Thank you."

He leans against a crate. "What is your part in all of this?"

I reach my hands to my head and pull the note out of my braid and then hand it to him.

His face tightens as he reads it, and then he hands back the page. "I won't let you do this."

"Yes, you will. Please."

He snaps his head back and throws his arms forward, his muscles tensing. "I'd be murdering my own princess."

"No, you would be helping me and protecting our people."

"And if this doesn't go the way you plan? They kill you and our men?"

A crate creaks as the ship dips to the side on a wave. I watch a spider spinning a web in a far corner. "I don't know. I can only trust that God has my life in His hands." I turn back to him and venture forward on my knees. "I can't do this without you. I need you to do this for me. I'm telling you to. Please, trust me."

He runs his hands through his hair as his gaze rises to the ceiling and then back to me. "You're certain you are willing to do this?"

"I'm certain."

He looks at me for a minute in silence. "Lord Ashton is like a second father to me. He is being held in that beast of a king's dungeon along with the rest of them." A heavy sigh pushes from his lips. "So I will do this for you, for my loyalty to him, and for our country."

Ignoring propriety, I grab his hand. "For those men and our country. Thank you, Eldon."

He runs his hand though his hair again. Standing up, he moves to the other side of the crate and slides down.

I reach into my cloak, open one of the bags and pull out my wet Bible. Prying open the soaked pages, I place it atop a crate and then pull my cloak tighter around me. Laying my head back, I let out a long breath. Eldon's breathing on the other side of the crate times with the waves lapping onto the shore outside.

I close my eyes.

CHAPTER 13

"Make ready for port!"

I free my arms from beneath my cloak. Yes, I heard correctly. We're only minutes from Alandar.

A grumble from my stomach separates the silence. I wrap my arm around my middle and look at the empty leather bag next to me that was filled with food only yesterday. Eldon groans as he shifts his back against a crate.

I turn to the window. Grainy clouds crowd a sky colored faint purple with evening. Pressing my lips, I breathe out. This is it.

As I try to change position, my back groans. I lean forward and rub my hands over my shoulders, pushing my fingers into the knots that clump there. Hunger scratches my stomach. Fatigue pulls at my eyelids from a night of uncomfortable and broken sleep. I twist forward as a broken crate edge jags into my lower back, and I round my lips as a sigh rushes out. Getting out of this box will be pure heaven.

Yet until protection comes in the form of night, I'll still be confined. I fumble to my feet, lean over one of the crates, and stare out the window. Alandar's shoreline reaches for miles, inviting rolling wave after wave.

A jerk pushes me backward. I stumble against a crate and grab its edge. The harbor. I glance down at Eldon, his back slumped against a barrel and his arms resting on his knees. He lifts his head and looks back at me.

Hours later, I watch the sun slink to its home, Eldon on a barrel next to me. Streaks of pink, red, orange, and yellow stretch across the sky. The clouds drift through the colors like painted cotton balls.

Eldon's whisper barely stirs the air. "Dark is our cue to leave the ship, I assume."

"Yes."

As the dark finally rolls in, I slide off the crate and grasp my Bible, placing it in the leather bag. Then I secure the note back in the upper part of my braid and fasten the leather bag with the rope within my cloak. Eldon stuffs the empty leather food bag behind a crate in a corner of the room while I make sure the bag with the Bible and the penses are firm within my folds.

We then squeeze through the cargo maze and make our way to the door. I lean my ear against the wood and listen. Nothing. Taking a deep breath and sending up a silent prayer, I open the door and creep out, Eldon closing it behind me.

Eerie shadows fill the air, playing around faint light slithering down from above. After crossing to the trapdoor, I watch Eldon slowly climb the wooden ladder to the top to push it open. He nods at me and crawls out. I clasp the iron bars and pull myself upward.

Shivering as the chilly night breeze sweeps around me, I scan the ship. No movement disturbs the black of the night. I cross to the railing where Eldon is and peer over. Sailors line the docks, their sluggish shouts, curses, and drawls spilling into the night. Few people walk the village's streets.

I look up. The Alandarin palace hovers in the darkness, leering over everything like a dark claw.

I turn and hurry to the other railing and lean over. Dark water swirls beneath me. Eldon and I nod at each other, and he swings his leg around and crawls down. I can barely hear the stir in the water. Looking down at him, he again nods. I grasp the railing, my hands gripping so hard my knuckles turn white, and lift one leg over. Wiggling my feet into the net, I ease myself down.

A wave rolls beneath the ship. My foot slides over the mesh. My grip slips with it, and I fall, crashing into the black water and Eldon as he tries to catch me. The icy nip of the water jabs my body as my breath hangs in midair. My throat stings with the salt water I gulped down.

The sailors' prattle grows louder. The beating inside my chest races to a drum's marching pace. Crouching lower into the freezing water, I wait ... and wait ...

The noise fades. Eldon helps me up, and we wade to the side of the boat.

"I told ye I heerd somthin'!" a cracked voice hollers.

We press ourselves against the boat, alarm stabbing my chest and silent prayers drifting upward.

"No, ye dint," another voice follows. "Yee're jist drunk."

A jumbled mess of voices rise. Hardly daring to breathe, I wade through the water, crouched low, not stopping until my feet meet dry ground.

Eldon creeps inches ahead of me, and after a quick glance at me, he whips over to the shelter of a tree. A few minutes of silence pass. I straighten and dart to his cover.

"Hey, did ye see that? Somethin' moved o'er there."

"Shore did. I saw it wit' me own eyes."

My chest tightens. Eldon and I shrink deeper into the shadow of the tree. Heavy feet move across the ground.

"It was right o'er here," a husky voice declares.

My heart pounds with dread. The sailors come closer and closer ...

Eldon grabs my arm and jerks me from the tree. I run as fast as I can go, not looking back.

"Ay! There they go!"

I don't stop. I run and run, the wind bringing tears to my eyes as I search for someplace to hide. My one focus blots out everything else as shadows whiz past me. A tall thicket of trees and bushes appear in the distance. I streak into the concealment, throwing my hands over my face against the branches.

Behind me, the only sound that sweeps across my ears is the brisk night breeze. I drop my head and gulp in air. *Thank You, Jesus. Thank You.*

Eldon. I strain to see through the gloom. Though I assumed he followed, not even a moving shadow catches my eye. Behind me, about ten yards away, the Alandarin castle looms. I inch out on my knees. The wind whisks through my hair.

A twig snaps, and a shadow moves in a thick gathering of pines. I lean forward. The square, broad shoulders and thick arms tell me I've found him. I stand up and run for the pines. Just as I reach the trees, Eldon reaches out and pushes my shoulders to the ground then drops down beside me.

"You all right?" I can barely hear his whisper.

I nod. "You?"

"Fine. What now?"

"You deliver the message."

"God protect us."

"He will."

I reach into my cloak and bring out my pouch. I take my Bible from among the penses and then give the pouch to Eldon. "You'll need money while you're here." I then reach up to my braid and pull out the note. I read over it one more time.

King Maurice,

The twenty-four lords and knights whom you now hold are worth nothing to you. As the sole heir to His Royal Highness, King Norman, and as the future queen of Aundria, I ask that you spare their lives and grant them their freedom and safe passage back to Aundria. In return, I will willingly give myself to you to do with as you see fit.

My terms are simple. Send three of your soldiers to bring out the twenty-four hostages. My servant will lead them to a meeting place. Once I am certain of the knights' and lords' safety, I will return alone with your three soldiers. If even one more soldier is brought with them, I will not come out of hiding, and the terms between us will be broken.

Royal Princess Lorelle of Aundria

Eldon carefully takes the note from me as I secure my Bible with the rope beneath my cloak again.

"You are sure?" Eldon asks gently.

"I'm sure."

He takes my hand in his and places a gentle kiss on it. "God be with you, Princess."

I touch his arm in response. "And you, Eldon. Thank you."

A small smile surfaces on his face. "For Aundria."

"For Aundria."

He stands up out of our hiding place and walks to the huge iron gates surrounding the Alandarin palace.

Please, Jesus. Keep us safe. Thank You for bringing us this far.

Eldon's broad back grows smaller and smaller as the distance between us grows. His footsteps crunch on the ground, slowly fading into the night. A fly buzzes in my ear. I flick it away as a branch jags into my neck. A coyote howls across the mountains.

Then silence. Silence louder than anything I've ever heard.

I pull my knees to my chest, tucking my chin in between them.

"What do you want?" a deep, gruff voice says.

I can't make out Eldon's next words, but I see him moving his hands and showing the letter to a soldier with a beard as red as blood. Thick silence squeezes the air. The soldier nods and swings open the gate. It swallows Eldon in as it shuts behind him.

I turn and crawl through the thicket, away from the castle. Once I'm through the thicket, I stand up and scan the trees. A few yards ahead of me I see the one I need—huge and wide, with thick multiple branches.

I grasp a branch and pull myself up. Higher and higher I climb, twigs snagging my skin, until the branches become too far apart to climb any more. But perfect to hide me.

I lay my head against the tree's trunk to wait and pray, listening to the leaves swish and rustle over my skin, the faint hoot of an owl far off in the night, and the night wind whispering around me.

My hair lifts off my shoulders as a shiver runs through my body. I hug myself tighter. A squirrel jumps to a branch above me, sniffing the air and swaying with the wind. Another coyote howls in the distance. The moon shines a dusty light through the gray clouds.

The creak of the iron gate pierces the air. I lift my head. Faint footsteps sound in the night. Leaves crunch under heavy boots. I look toward the palace and see them, a group of men tied together by one rope, led by four others. I count twenty-eight men total.

About a yard away from my tree, the group stops. One of them steps out. Eldon.

"Your Highness, King Maurice has accepted your terms. I am here with the twenty-four lords and knights and three Alandarin soldiers," Eldon says loudly.

I puff out a breath. Twigs snap beneath me as I make my way down. When I reach the bottom, I turn and look at the group of men. Their faces tell me seeing a princess climb out of a tree is not an everyday occurrence.

"I am Princess Lorelle. You are King Maurice's soldiers?"

"You are correct," a man answers in a deep voice. He walks toward me as another soldier begins untying the knights.

I look at Eldon. He faintly nods.

A second soldier steps beside me with the rope and ties my wrists together. Bright moonlight fills the woods. I look up to see a gap in the clouds.

A figure steps out of the group of knights into the moonlight. I turn back, knowing what I will see. Scars and bruises cover his face—a thinner, weaker face. My neck tenses.

"Lorelle?" Sir Wellington whispers.

"All right, we're ready," the soldier says as he grasps my upper arm and starts walking.

"Wait—" Sir Wellington reaches out and grabs my other arm. His eyes lock onto mine, the concern in them so hot I feel as if it burns into me.

The soldier yanks me, but Sir Wellington's grip only tightens. "What are you doing?"

I just look at him, trying to tell him a thousand things without saying anything at all.

Another soldier pushes Sir Wellington's shoulder. "Let her go, young man. She's coming with us now."

Realization mixed with horror flicks across the knight's features. He pulls me toward him, his clasp almost hurting me.

"I can't let her go." He pulls his anguish-filled gaze to the soldier holding me. "Take me. Please, take me in her place … anything …"

This time the soldier succeeds in tearing me from Sir Wellington's grasp. The other soldier shoves Sir Wellington, but Sir Wellington pushes him to the side.

The soldier holding me smirks. "You think a cheap knight like you is worth the value of a princess?"

I almost lose my balance as he jerks me into a walk. My gaze clings to Sir Wellington as I'm moved farther away, his eyes burning back into mine. As he starts to follow me, another Aundrian knight reaches out and grasps his arm, holding him back. The pain that covers his face cuts into my heart like a knife slicing into my flesh.

A cluster of trees hides him from me as the soldiers pull me farther away. My eyes burn. Swallowing feels like forcing down clumps of jagged rocks. I can still feel him behind me.

When we reach the gates, a soldier on the inside unlocks and swings them open. I step inside, and he slams it shut behind me, the clash deafening in the night.

"Follow me," the dark voice commands. I walk behind him, the other soldiers forming a line behind me until we reach the throne room.

The doors sweep open. His eyes locked on me, King Maurice sits on the tall throne, his hands curled over the chair's sides. The soldiers stop when we reach him.

"Your Majesty, Princess Lorelle of Aundria," one of the soldiers announces.

Staring into King Maurice's eyes, I ease my shoulders down. Fresh hatred from the unspeakable pain he has caused me begins to simmer in my stomach, but I breathe in and lift my chin again. He doesn't have the hope I have.

A grin pulls his lips. His fingertips stroke his bony chin. "At last I see you again." A low laugh rumbles through his chest. "Welcome back to Alandar."

I don't move.

"I think trading in twenty-four worthless lords and knights for a princess isn't a bad deal at all."

He leans further out of his chair and closer to me. "Are you willing to throw yourself back into my dungeon?"

"I am."

A cruel smile spreads itself across his face. "You are brave, Princess Lorelle. Very brave indeed."

My tongue curls inside my mouth. His green eyes dig into me. I remember those green eyes.

"I will look forward to seeing you again, Princess." Looking up at the soldiers behind me, he nods and sinks his back against the chair. "Take her away."

Soldiers grasp my arms and pull me away. Straightening my shoulders, I smile a little. Sir Wellington is free.

Instead of taking the route to the dungeons below, the soldiers turn and bring me down a long stone hallway. One soldier stops at a door, disappears into the room behind it as we wait, and then emerges seconds later with a lit lantern and a key. We continue walking, and seconds pass before the soldiers open another door in the wall and lead me up a steep staircase. Minutes later my feet ache from climbing.

At the top, we step into a gray stone hallway, where faint moonlight throws in thin shadows from a barred window in the far wall. A winding staircase next to the window twists upward through a hole in the hall's ceiling. I look up as they bring me to the foot of the staircase. I can't even see the top in the darkness.

They pull me forward, and we begin the upward trek. Our footsteps clatter in the silence. Where are they taking me?

The cold presses my damp clothes firmer around my body, and a shiver snaps in my shoulders. I peer into the dark, where the lantern's flickering flame casts elongated shadows onto walls far away, like ghosts stretching and then shrinking.

A black ceiling looms above us. As we draw closer, an etched-out square of a trapdoor comes into view. When we reach it, a soldier presses his back against it, and it pops open. After untying my wrists, he grabs me and lifts me through the opening, setting me on the floor next to the hole. Then he pulls the door shut, and the soldiers are gone.

A sharp wind slams into me. I catch myself on my hands.

One round stone wall surrounds me, broken up by two huge, widely barred windows. The ceiling curves into a deep cone above me. A tower.

I pull myself to my feet, my hands damp from pressing against the stone floor beneath me. The trapdoor has no handle or hole. It's just a slab of rock, completely impossible to open from my side. I rub my hands over my arms and look around the room.

Completely empty, the tower is small, enough to hold only me and possibly two or three other people. As another blast of wind flaps my dress out behind me, I walk to the window. The spaces between the black bars are large but not large enough for me to crawl through. Yet as I look down, any idea of escape whisks away with the wind.

The ground sits hundreds of feet below me. My tower stands far away from any others of the castle, isolated in the cold air. Miles of Alandarin valleys, mountains, forests, and villages stretch before me. The Jasmin Sea, silver beneath a full moon, crashes its waves together. I can see everything.

Sir Wellington's pleading face, his eyes bright with emotion, appears in my mind. I swallow as my gut tightens.

Eldon will protect them. The penses I gave him will last him and the rest of them until they can go home. *Please, King Jesus. Protect them.*

I wrap my hands around the icy bars and stare out of my prison at the moon, cold and white above the world below me.

111

CHAPTER 14

Thunder crashes. Lightning cracks through the sky. A blast of icy wind sweeps in another shower of water, soaking me further. I wipe the drops from my eyelashes and wrap my arms tighter around myself.

My teeth chatter too hard to rest my chin on my knees. Looking up, I rub my hands over my face and feel them shaking. The windows are too large and the bars too thin to hold in the swoops of rainy wind.

My stomach twists as it gurgles with hunger again. I look at the empty water jug and bowl of mush beside me. The past day I haven't been able to force myself to eat it after finding a rat tail inside. Now, I am desperate. I grasp the bowl and shove a spoonful into my mouth. Bitter juice with hard chunks fills my mouth. I gag and spit it back out.

My stomach rumbles again as another roar of thunder claps next to the tower, rain rushing through the huge windows and needling my face. If I don't eat that mush, I'll starve. I squeeze my eyes shut and thrust it into my mouth.

<hr />

I don't bother to open my eyes. My body shakes too hard, even though my dress sticks to my body with sweat. Two weeks of icy rain, piercing winds, and bad food or no food at all isn't agreeing with me. The question is, how much longer will I last?

I let myself fall back into a gray sleep. An image of my mother dying, soaked in blood, tears across my mind. I scream and shoot my eyes open.

Footsteps pound on the stairs below the trapdoor. I pull myself up to my elbows and strain my ears, dizziness swirling in my head.

Seconds later the door bursts open and King Maurice's top advisor, Lord Durwin Cardon, stands up in the hole. He reaches forward, grabs my ankle, and yanks me toward him. I let out a cry of surprise as I drop through the opening into his arms. He wraps his huge arm around my waist, carrying me like a plank, and rushes down the dark stairs.

"All right, you, you're coming with me!" His guttural voice pounds my ears. Malice slimes over his words as he barks, "Aundria will now see who has the power. Oh, yes, they will see. And they will regret what they've done and are doing!"

He reaches the bottom, charges through the open door, and hurries down the second flight of stairs. I try to kick my feet against him, but his grasp is locked. After running down another hallway, he turns and pulls me into a small, candlelit room lined with swords, knives, and spears. He thrusts me down onto the ground and marches over to a collection of knives. A rock falls in my stomach.

Get out, get out!

My hands and feet struggle over the floor like weights as I try to escape out the door, but he grabs my dress and yanks me back. His arm wraps around my neck. I cough and gasp as he raises a knife in the air, its silver blade glistening in the candlelight.

I kick and send my curled first plunging into his face. He winces, his raised arm weakening for a second and his grip on me loosening. I punch him a second time and drive my leg back into his stomach. Agonized groans fly from his mouth, and I take the opportunity to lunge for his hand that holds the knife and grasp it, struggling to lower it.

His knee thrusts into my back and he tightens his clasp around my neck, raising the knife above my reach. I squirm and writhe, my eyes squeezing shut. Gasping and gagging, I grope for his arm.

A yell of pain tears through the air. The clutch around my neck loosens as his body falls backward, taking me with him. Gagging, I turn my head and stare at the blood gushing from his side. His eyes are frozen open.

Two hands grasp me and gently lift me up. Too weak to fight anymore, I fall against the person's frame. Bright blue eyes gaze into mine. I open my mouth in shock, but my weak legs slip out from under me. Sir Wellington catches me and picks me up in his arms.

"What—what are you doing here?" My voice cracks as the words come out.

A smile spreads across his face. "I came for you."

I swing my head to the doorway, searching for any other soldiers. "But—what's happening?"

"Either Alandar or Aundria ends tonight," he answers. "We and Julinar have waged a surprise attack." His gaze softens. "Are you all right?"

As I numbly open my mouth to speak, I feel as if all the blood is sucked from my head and down to my stomach. I drop my head on his shoulder.

He kneels down with me in his arms and feels my forehead. His brow creases. "You're ill, seriously ill." He sweeps my hair out of my face.

The clash of swords rings in the air. We spin toward the doorway.

"Stay here." He draws his sword and, with one last glance at me, darts out of the room.

His footsteps pound down the hall, toward the chilling noises. I sit for a minute, dizzy and shaking, as the wrenching sounds fade farther and farther away.

The prisoners.

I drag myself up, tremors still rippling through my body, and venture a few steps. The walls spin, and my eyes blur. I blink and stumble to the collection of keys hanging on the wall. I grasp the one I saw used during my first stay in the Alandarin dungeons and pull myself from the room.

The darkness and chill of the hallway swallows me. Dead soldiers lie in crumpled heaps at my feet. I gulp and slip my fingers into the hand of Jesus. Strength plunges through me as I haul myself as fast I can toward the throne room. Once I reach it, I stop, searching for the way to the dungeons below. I recognize a hallway I was dragged through before and make my way forward.

Remembering a door in the wall with a staircase leading down to the cells, I fumble around until I find it and then pull it open. At the bottom of the staircase, I open the second door and almost fall as I stumble through.

The same pungent smell stings my nose. Cells line the walls ahead of me.

I untangle my skirt from my foot and grope to the first cell. A frightened voice filters through the bars. "Who's that?"

"A friend," I reply. I grasp onto the bars for support and then fumble the key into the lock. "You're free," I whisper to the unseen prisoner. "Now go!"

A dark figure pushes the door open and stumbles out of the cell. He searches for my hand and clasps it. "Thank you, thank you," he mumbles before disappearing into the black.

I pat the walls until I find the next cell. After sliding the door open, I bid the captive to leave. He slips past me and is gone.

I go to cell after cell, unlocking the doors and freeing the Julinarin captives and anyone else being kept in this unforgiving pit where with the smallest word, the king can throw someone down to his or her death.

Words of thanks drift past my ears as the prisoners run free. Finally, my hands hit a dirt wall. I've unlocked every cell.

Where are Betsy and Martin? Still in the slave quarters?

I move back down the way I came. Fatigue grips me. My throat aches, and fever wracks my body. I have to get to them. I stumble forward, my eyes stinging and my ears pounding. One more step ...now another ... *Keep going, Lorelle. Keep going*, I think.

The underground air chills my fingers as I stretch my arms out in front of me, fumbling down the dirt passage. At the end, I clasp the metal door's handle and pull it open. The black hallway home to the slaves stretches in front of me. The doors lining the walls are all open. Silence pinches the air.

Empty.

I turn and leave the hallway and come to the door leading to the stairway. A faint beam of light slithers from the top of the steps. I stagger forward and pull my feet over each stair.

At the top, I squint against the light. Yes, this is a hallway I've been down before. The candles, weapons, and armor lining the walls are all too recognizable. I slide my hand along the wall to steady me as I make my way down, silence splitting my ears. When I reach the end, I stop short.

Steps have been torn off staircases, railings have been smashed or removed, adornments have been thrown to the ground, and heaps and heaps of stones cover the floor. I swallow bile in my throat. Dead soldiers, knights, and lords splatter the floor, some partially covered by the rocks.

I stare around me, trying to look over the bodies. How to get out? Ragged holes fill the walls. Perhaps I could climb out through one of them ... I start toward one, choking on the thick, gray dust in the air. When I finally reach the wall, I grab it and pull myself through.

The surprise that awaits me on the other side steals my breath. Bodies cover the field in front of the castle, lifeless horses and blood surrounding them. I struggle forward, scanning the battlefield. And then I see them ... I recoil, hardly daring to breathe, to move ...

King Maurice and my father lie in the distance in crumpled heaps. Blood clings to their armor and spills across the ground.

CHAPTER 15

My heart rises to my throat. I stagger toward my father and King Maurice, my breath caught in my chest. "No, no ..."

Horse hooves sound in the distance. I try to run, try to keep my eyes on my father, but my legs weigh me down like bricks. My eyes blur, but I need to keep going. I need to keep going ...

"Your Highness, stop!" Muffled words drift over my head.

Two hands grasp me. My feet slip from the ground as the person swings me up into his arms and begins to run. I try looking into the person's eyes but see only a crown of brown hair and a blurred face.

I moan and push at the stranger, but his grasp on me only tightens. I spin my head around, searching for my father.

"Help me get her to the ship. Quickly!"

"King Norman! Over here!"

Father ... Father ...

My chest tightens. Heat scourges my cheeks. Pieces of glass seem to cluster in my throat. My forehead threatens to split apart from the pounding in my head. I struggle to keep my eyes open, but seconds later everything goes black.

I pull the blankets closer to my face and burrow deeper into the pillow. A satin bedspread brushes my chin. The smell of tobacco and spice tickles my nose.

Light kisses my eyes as sleep drifts away. Where am I? I crack open an eyelid. A large room with rich wood walls meets my gaze. Glass windows with gold panes grace one wall, and a small chandelier hangs in the middle of the ceiling. A dark wood desk stands in the center of another wall, and a red sofa leans on the opposite side.

I rub a hand over my cheek. Cool skin meets my fingers. My eyes don't blur the furniture in front of me. My held feels as light as the feathers that cover some of the pillows around me. No sweat or shivers swallow my body.

Father.

I shoot up, whip off the blanket, and jump off the bed. As soon as my feet hit the floor, hunger pierces my stomach. I pull myself to the window, my throat tightening. Miles and miles of swishing water meet my eyes.

A rock drops in my gut. Where on earth am I headed? I squeeze my eyes shut and search for reminiscences of the night before. Faded scenes of the destroyed castle, dark hallways, and prisoners come creeping back, yet something stops them from coming all the way.

I can remember nothing else, except the image of my father lying crumpled on the ground, bloodstained and motionless. A flood of tears rushes to my eyes. I cover my mouth and sink to the floor.

I don't know how long I sit there, curled in a ball beneath the window, head throbbing and eyes burning. This. It's come to this. Weeks and weeks of holding out to see him, and when we finally were near each other, death stepped in again and seared another burn into me. I will never be able to tell him I love him again.

When I have nothing left to cry, I bury my head in my lap and let the world steal my senses.

I finally lift my head and draw in a long, shuddering breath. Dried tears chap my cheeks. I run my hands under my eyes and then look toward the window. Golden sunlight breaks through clouds and shimmers through the glass.

I clutch my middle and stand up, trying to swallow my hunger. My eyes catch a gold centerpiece sitting on the desk at the other side of the room. "Captain Drake Carrington" is etched in the center of the gold.

Captain Drake Carrington? The … the captain of the ship that took me from Alandar to Julinar. Relief eases back my shoulders. I know I'm safe with him. But still—where am I going? Julinar?

A soft tapping jerks my head toward the door. I blink at the frame and shift my feet. "Come."

The door slides open. Bright blue eyes peer forth.

I just stand there, hugging myself, not even wanting to speak.

His gaze remains fastened on me for a moment, and then he lowers himself in a bow. Scars and bruises cover his face. "Your Highness."

Words try to form on my tongue, but my heart only threatens to jump there instead.

"How do you feel?" He seems to be fumbling, his eyes on me one minute and on the floor the next.

I rub my hands up and down my arms. "I still feel shaky, but I think my fever is gone."

He takes a step toward me. "Yes, your fever broke late last night. You've been sleeping for two days straight."

I stare at him. "Two days? I thought it was just last night I collapsed."

No wonder hunger stabs my stomach and my throat burns. And if we have already been at sea for two days, then we should have reached Julinar by now. Does that mean I am finally going home?

"The battle. What was the battle's end?" I hug myself tighter.

His gentle smile spreads to his eyes. "Aundria has won."

My breath snaps. "We've won?"

"We've won."

I fall back against the wall. All the longing I've had for the war to end, and now it stands before me, finished. Aundria, free from the oppression and pain of Alandar. I struggle to process a fact that seems so unreal but so beautiful.

"The battle was the closest one we've had yet," he continues, taking another step into the room, "but we succeeded. We still have forces back in Alandar helping the Alandarin people."

I brush my hand over the wall. What will life hold for me now that the war is over? Will things be the same again? Or will everything be drastically different, even more different than everything was after the start of the war changed it?

Father. His death will change my life forever. I press my hand against my chest as my body begins to shake with hunger. My other arm hugging my stomach, I stumble back to my bed and nearly collapse on it.

His eyes lock with mine. "Stay here." And he disappears out the door.

I lean back on my bed. Another bubble of emotion rises in my throat. I shut my eyes and bite my cheek.

Father, dead. I never had the chance to share with him what Jesus has done for me, yet I know what his response would have been: cold, stubborn, and unwilling. He always taught me to respect Aundria's bishop, but he himself only acted in the compelled part of religion and urged me not to go any further. And now he would never know how much further he could have really gone.

The door opens wider. Sir Wellington, along with a woman, steps into the room with trays of steaming food and drink. I drag myself up and to the edge of the bed.

After a quick bob, the woman hands me a tray laden with plates and bowls filled with meat, bread, and soup. Sir Wellington silently hands me a glass of water. I drink, the cool water so sweet and refreshing the glass empties too quickly. Once I finish, I brush my hand across my lips.

"Thank you. I appreciate it."

The woman turns and leaves, but Sir Wellington stays, gaze fixed on me, still standing by the bed. I want him to leave … want so badly to just be alone … yet why do I also want him to stay with me?

He kneels down beside the bed, quiet and avoiding eye contact. I set the glass down on the sheets when he finally breaks the silence. "A duel with King Maurice has left your father suffering from a serious wound. King Maurice was killed."

I clap my hand to my throat. My mouth drops in amazement and relief as I stare at him. For a moment my tongue can't form any words. "My father is … alive?"

He rubs his chin. "Barely. He's unconscious right now. The ship's physician operated on him."

But he's alive.

I shift my gaze to the window, joy and relief enfolding me as I see my father's brown eyes flash before me, sparkling and laughing while his arms reach out to love me. So many months, so many agonized hours of longing for him, and now he is only rooms away from me.

I flip back the edge of the blanket. "Take me to him."

"You need food first. Here." He sets the plate on my bed.

I drag my legs over the bed's side. "No, please. I can't wait."

He braces his hands on my knees. "You probably can't even walk to his room by yourself."

"I'll be fine. You can support me." I start to stand up, but he rises with me and catches my shoulders, stopping me midair.

"No, you won't. I won't let you leave until you eat something."

I tilt my chin. With him standing there and holding me like that and my knees shaking under me from pure lack of food, there is definitely no way I will make it past him without eating first.

I drop back on the bed. "Fine. Hand me the fork."

The pork, bread, and soup numb the pain in my stomach as my hunger slowly subsides. Strength trickles back into my body.

"We should arrive in Aundria in a little less than a week," he says, kneeling down beside me.

I stop chewing. "Then I'm finally going home?"

He barely nods, a smile pulling at his lips. "You're going home."

I set down the fork and press my hand against my cheek, overwhelmed with everything I've heard since I woke up. *Thank You, Lord. Thank You.* God has been faithful. After all this time, He is leading me back.

"Your Highness," Sir Wellington begins, rubbing his hands over his arms, "thank you—for getting me out of that cold, dark dungeon. Their treatment toward me there was absolutely foul, and I was becoming uncertain how long I would last. You came just in time."

A small smile creeps over me. "I'm glad you are safe."

He shifts his position. "Did you go and shoot the night of the Alandarin attack?" Genuine curiosity shines in his eyes.

A warm blush spreads across my face. "I did. And broke a leg and sprained the other."

He leans back and breathes out. "You don't let anything stop you, do you?"

I look up at him. "How could I when the lives of those I care about were at stake? Besides, God was beside me the entire time."

His blue eyes hold mine. "He will never leave us or forsake us."

I smile. "No."

"Finished?" He nods toward my plate. I nod and set it on the bed. He offers his arm, and I loop mine through it. I relish being able to stand without my knees shaking.

He leads me down a narrow hallway. At the end of it, he raises his fist and knocks on a wooden door as my thoughts swirl. Am I prepared for this moment? Am I prepared for what I am about to see?

The door opens, revealing a short, slim man with a pointy beard and curled mustache. Black hair tinted with gray wraps around his head, and gray eyes that look too small for his face peak out from beneath heavy eyebrows.

Sir Wellington places a hand on my shoulder. "Doctor Adams, may I present Her Highness, Princess Lorelle of Aundria."

The Edge of Redemption

The man's eyes widens as he lowers himself in a bow. "Your Highness, do come in. The king has just awakened."

I nod and slip past the doctor and Sir Wellington as they both leave the cabin, which is very similar to mine. In the corner, my father lies on a bed, his bandaged arm and leg resting on two piles of pillows.

Tears welling in my eyes, I rush over to his side and drop to my knees next to the bed. A faint smile lights up his face as we clasp each other's hands. "My dear daughter."

His gentle brown eyes look into mine, so tired but so full of love. I reach out and stroke his cheek, joy and grief crashing together inside me.

"Oh, I've missed you! I've missed you every second of every day! Are you all right?" I ask.

"Getting by." His husky voice struggles. Never before in my life have I seen him so helpless and aged. His face droops with fatigue. "Look at you! Tears running all over the place."

I laugh and wipe my fingers under my eyes.

"You've grown up since the time I last saw you," he says. I squeeze his hand tighter. His fingers linger in my hair. "You're absolutely beautiful. My, you look just like your mother."

My other hand joins my first in clasping his. I lower my voice to almost a whisper. "How are you, really?"

His gaze wanders to his bandaged arm. "Well, I'm not young anymore, that's certain." He turns back to me. "The pain has been hard to cope with, but I'm getting by. This old body of mine is surely wearing."

"You were injured," I reply, switching my gaze to his thickly bandaged leg.

"And now I'm sick and weak," he answers as a sigh heavy as iron pushes through his lips.

I swallow and lay my hand on his bandaged arm. "You've won."

A smile breaks through. "We've won. And we're on our way home."

I smile and kiss his hand.

God has been faithful.

I run a finger over his bandaged leg. "What—what happened to your leg?"

"I broke it."

I tip my head. "How?"

"Never you mind," he answers, patting my cheek. "It just happened during the battle."

I look back at the bandages.

His finger gently touches my chin. I turn back and look at him.

"My daughter, how are you? You've been through a great deal, and you've grown up so much. Every minute, every second, every day was spent thinking of you. What has this war done to you? What has happened to my little girl?" He reaches out and rubs his fingers over my cheek.

I curl my hands around one of his wrists. "I'm right here. I—I've never been hurt more than I could bear." I swallow and grip his hand harder. "Father, while we were apart, I made a discovery." Any approaching nerves back away at the thought that I almost lost him, and this is my second chance. "A glorious discovery."

"What, my child?"

I move my hands to one of his and slide them over his rough skin, back and forth. "I discovered … the power of God's never-ending love and forgiveness."

His features harden for a moment. His eyes switch to the window, but they return in a moment. "Lorelle, don't foolishly dive into something worthless and empty."

"Faith in the Lord is not foolish, Father," I answer. "It's fulfilling and promising and strengthening. God … He offers amazing supplies of love, joy, peace, and strength. And He promises eternal life."

A snort escapes his lips. "Eternal life? You know no such thing exists."

"I believe with my whole heart it does."

He pushes up from the bed with a sigh—almost a groan. "Oh, Lorelle, we've talked about this. Don't commit your life to something that will desert you in the end."

"Do you have any evidence that it will?"

"Let me ask you this," he answers instead. "Do you have any evidence that God exists?"

"I do," I reply, lifting my chin. "The Bible."

"And you're going to base your beliefs and life on one book of many."

"It's not just any book," I answer. "It's God's Word, and it has stood unshakably for thousands of years." I think back to the conversation months ago between Sir Wellington and myself. "Father, any creative storybook can give a person a sensation. But this Book—this Book gives peace and joy and strength. It lifts you up even when you're in the darkest pit. It refreshes you and restores you and—"

"All right, enough." His words are almost curt. "If it will please you, I'll think on it for a while, but I didn't want you to come in here to bore me with religion. I want to hear about *you*, my daughter. How have you been doing?"

That was it? I knew he would be against it, but to want to leave the topic so quickly ... disappointment stings me. "Uh, getting by, like you said, though I haven't gone through the past months without a few scars."

He tucks a curl behind my ear. "I'm so sorry for what you've had to go through. If I could wipe away all the pain you've experienced, I would before you could even blink." A smile creeps back to his face. "Oh, how I've missed you."

I lean closer and kiss his cheek then press mine against his. "Don't ever let me leave you again."

I suddenly feel like the little girl I used to be, clinging to her father, wanting to sit on his lap. I hug him tighter and shut my eyes, praying he will be all right.

Chapter 16

Daybreak brings a new hope, a relief from the sorrow the conversation with my father caused the day before. I leave my cabin and walk across the main deck to the ship's railing, thankful for the fresh air that fills my lungs. The water splashes and dances like millions of tiny mermaids as the sun sparkles down its light. My hair whisks out behind me with the sea breeze. I relax my face, shut my eyes, and let the beauty sink in.

"Your Highness?"

I turn at the deep, rumbling voice. Captain Carrington stands next to me. "Captain Carrington." I smile. "It is a pleasure to see you again."

He grins and graces me with an elegant bow. "I am relieved to see you recovered and healthy."

I wrap one of my curls around my finger. "Yes, thank you. I am feeling much better." I laugh inside at the thought of how every time I am on a ship those words seem to come out of my mouth.

"You were quite frail when we brought you aboard the ship," he says. "You held us all in worry."

I laugh. "Well, do accept my apology. But I do thank you, Captain Carrington, for giving me your cabin. Now that I am recovered, perhaps you will allow me to return it to you. A smaller room downstairs would be perfectly adequate."

Hesitation shows on his face. "But you are still slightly weak."

I wave a hand through the air. "As long as I have a bed, I'll be fine."

I can see the spark in his eyes. "Very well, Your Highness. It will be done. Now if you will allow me, may I inquire about your father?"

I lower my head to study the weathered planking beneath my feet. "He's all right, though still very weak."

"Well, I trust Doctor Adams," he says. "He'll take care of him well and efficiently. Now if you'll excuse me, I must be getting back to work."

He bows and then walks away with long, heavy strides. I turn and stare into the tossing waves, my fingers gripping the railing. My gut twists into a knot as thoughts of my father linger in my mind. He will heal, won't he?

A hand covers mine. My heart jumps as Sir Wellington smiles at me. "Hello," I whisper, a strange wave of excitement splashing over me.

"Hello." He runs his free hand over the railing as his other tightens slightly around mine. "How are you doing?"

"I'm all right," I lie, ducking my face to hide any emotion that would show. But as his fingers wait on mine, I lift my head back up. "My father ..."

He turns his body to face me. "Your father is strong. He will push through these injuries."

I nod, pressing my lips together. Silence surrounds us as we both turn and look at the water.

"He's like you, Lorelle. He won't let anything beat him."

I smile at the hidden compliment, looking down at the railing as his encouragement eases the knot in my gut a little looser.

"Would you like to come to the forecastle deck with me?"

I squint in the sun as I turn toward him. "I would love to." I loop my arm in his before he even offers, and we walk across the main deck to the short stairs leading up to the forecastle deck. At the top, a salty spray sprinkles over me. I smile as he grins with me.

127

He spreads his fingers through his hair. "This is one of my favorite views. Hardly anything is between me and the sea and sky."

I take my arm out of his and walk farther across the deck, closer to the waves splashing against the hull below. Not a cloud above me. The sea, incredibly blue today because of the bright sky above, stretches to the horizon, where a thin, dark-blue line marks where water meets sky.

"I've always loved being on the sea," he says, walking up next to me. "It's so freeing."

I turn to him. "When was your first voyage?"

He wipes his hand over his brow. "When I was eleven, my father let me accompany him when he sailed to Julinar for business. It was one of the happiest times I had with him."

He pauses, squinting into the sun. I look at him for a moment, my head to the side. "You miss him, don't you?"

He turns to me. "Very much."

I move closer to him, thinking of my mother and the moments of incredible grief her death has caused. "Will it get easier?"

His gaze moves to the sky. "I don't think the pain will ever go away." After a minute, he looks back at me. "But I think it will become more bearable over time. By God's grace."

I nod. "But it hurts so deeply now."

He takes my hand in his. "I know. I think about him every day. And every day I feel it all over again." Weaving his fingers through mine, he blows out a sigh. "I wouldn't be able to endure it if God wasn't beside me."

I watch a mountain of white foam jump in the air from the water. He's right. If God wasn't here to comfort me, would I really be able to bear it?

At that moment the ship plunges into a wave, and I stumble and fall into his chest. He catches me and wraps his hands around my shoulders, holding me secure.

I look up to see him staring back at me. As the ship rolls down the wave, water floods the deck, drenching us. We both gasp and jump back, staring down at our soaked clothes.

Suddenly he's laughing, and I grab my middle and laugh with him, wiping my forehead with my other hand. Droplets slide down my lips and into my mouth, and salt melts into my tongue.

It feels good to laugh.

◄○►

Moonlight shimmers down through the window of my cabin and lays a silver finger on me. My wool blanket sticks to my shoulders with sweat. I kick it to the floor and blow out a long sigh. After minutes of staring at the ceiling, I roll onto my stomach and lay my head on my arms.

The sea is a dark-blue field, its surface spun and rolled by a tropical breeze. Stars twinkle above, glimmering on the crest of waves like snow. Everything looks so peaceful and serene.

I flop over and jump off my bed. The heat in the room sticks to my neck and back like my blanket as I cross to the door, open it, and creep out. I tiptoe down the hallway and up the few stairs leading to the main deck.

Once outside, I stop and let the fresh, salty air refresh me. Breathing in, I release a relaxed sigh. Up here, the sea, moon, and stars seem inches away from my fingers, so close I could grasp them and call them mine.

I walk to the railing, the water's mist cooling my skin. The waves rolling onto the side of the ship send splashes onto my hot face. A breeze ruffles my nightdress, lifting my hair off of my shoulders.

I gaze into the blur of sparkles. Home. The word chimes like a bell in my mind.

"Sightseeing again, are we?" Sir Wellington ducks around a coil of rope and strides the short distance to me.

I smile as I watch him approach. "It is a beautiful night."

He shifts his gaze to the water. "It is that. You must be excited to be home?"

"With every part of me. It's been so long."

"It certainly has been, Your Highness."

Quiet sweeps over the deck. I study his firm jaw, his broad shoulders, his thick chest, his muscular arms. "I seem to recall you calling me by my first name once. Now you've changed to my formal title again."

A red hue sneaks into his cheeks. "Yes, well—"

"I don't mind," I interrupt. "Lorelle is just fine."

His eyes spark. "Then perhaps you could call me James."

I grin. "I'd be pleased to do so."

The splash of the waves against the ship echoes in the silence.

Shyly, he reaches out his arm and places it on my shoulders. My breath catches in my throat, and suddenly I relax into his gentle embrace.

"Oh, Lorelle, you've changed so much," he starts, a different tone in his voice. "You're so different than you were when I first met you."

I mull over his words for a minute. "I was such a snob."

He laughs and then quiets again. "You're becoming a beautiful young woman."

My heart jumps against my chest. He didn't sound casual yet not exactly admiring either—something I don't even dare to believe is there.

I look up into his blue eyes, my head spinning so fast I think it could fly into the night. He brings his hand to my hair and gently pushes a stray curl behind my ear.

"Wellington, come over here for a minute." The first mate's words sound like a wave crashing against the ship.

He shifts his feet, looking toward the first mate and then back to me. "Can I meet you here again tomorrow night?"

I breathe in a blast of salty air, trying to stop my smile from hurting my cheeks. "I'll be here."

James's hand touches my neck. "Good night, Lorelle," he whispers.

"Good night."

He reaches for my hand, kisses it, and is gone.

Little tingles race through my body and heat my neck. I stand staring at the spot where he just was, the tenderness I glimpsed in his blue eyes glued to my mind.

One last spray of seawater dampens my dress as I retreat downstairs. When I'm in my bedroom, I fall on the bed and flop my elbows on the pillow, chin in my hands.

James. His name twirls in my mind, warming my cheeks as I stare at the moon through my window.

I smile and bury my head in the pillow, tiny giggles slipping out.

Chapter 17

I have no trouble staying awake, waiting for the commotion of sailors to quiet on deck the next night. When all I can hear is the waves splashing against the ship's side outside my window, I swing my legs over my bed and sneak upstairs.

James turns from the railing and flashes a smile at me.

Inhaling the salty breeze, I walk over to him. "Have you been waiting long?"

"I would have waited all night."

I duck my head, grinning hard.

He takes my hand and leads me along the railing, pointing toward the sky. "Out here, the stars are incredible. This is one of my favorite parts of being on the sea."

I follow his finger. Millions of stars cover the sky. Each one glitters like a tiny snippet of the moon, creating a world of silver, sparkling light right above us. The waves glisten below as they splash around the ship.

Wrapping my hands tightly around the railing, I smile a sad smile. "She would have loved a night like this."

Placing his hands next to mine, he turns his head to me. "Who? Your mother?"

I look back up at the stars. "No, my sister."

"Your sister?"

"Yes, my sister, Claire."

He turns his body toward me. "You … you had a sister?"

I nod. "She was two years younger than me. She died when I was seven."

His forehead wrinkles. "How did she die?"

Facing him, I lean my head to the side. "I'm not sure you really want to know."

He takes a step closer to me. "You can tell me."

I turn back to the water. "It happened on a night when Alandarin warships were spotted at sea. She and my mother and I were sent off with soldiers to escape on foot through the forest behind the castle, to hide in the village of Shonemin on the other side."

I run a hand through my hair. The memory tastes bitter in my mouth.

"As we went, we eventually got separated into two groups. My mother and I were with some soldiers a bit ahead of the ones who had my sister. It wasn't long before Alandarin soldiers on horseback came after us, having somehow found out we were escaping through the woods. My mother and I were pulled into cover, but the Alandarins caught up with my sister and the soldiers with her. King Maurice was leading them."

A spray of saltwater springs over the railing. James reaches out and gently wipes away the droplets from my forehead.

"He ordered the Alandarin soldiers to bring Claire back to the castle, to make an example out of her." I swallow. "Then he drew his sword and killed her."

James grips the railing. I look down at the waves curling to the ship's side, their crests silver in the moonlight.

His fingers settle on mine. I turn to him, pressing my lips so hard they hurt.

"I'm so sorry. I'm so, so sorry."

I close my eyes as he pulls me into his embrace. Somehow, my shoulders feel looser, lighter, like a burden has been lifted from them, like I have released something that has been trapped inside me for a long time. It feels freeing.

I suddenly start smiling in his arms. Maybe it's from that feeling of release. I move my head to face his.

"I'm sure you didn't want me to come up here to tell you something as sad as that."

He only smiles a sad smile and brushes his hand over my cheek. "I'm glad you did. I would listen again."

He joins his other hand with the one at my cheek and cups my face. We both grow silent. I think my heart grows ten times in size.

He starts to bring his face closer to mine. I gulp in a breath and break out of his grasp, hurrying across the deck. Halfway across, I look back at him. He's still standing in the same place, staring at me, the wind ruffling his blond hair.

I rub a hand over my arm. "Come on. Let's go look at the other side."

As he starts to walk over to me, I turn and finish my cross to the opposite railing. The moon isn't straight above anymore on this side, so the waves appear darker and a deeper blue, not quite as silver as by the other railing.

James steps up next to me. I suck in a breath and look at him out of the corner of my eye then quickly look back to the sea.

Seconds of silence pass. A few yards away, a wave rolls over itself and splashes into a white foam.

"Look at how the water is a deep, pure blue on the surface, and below the waves, it's a dark, milky black." He points with his finger to the rippling ocean.

I look at him and then lean over to the water, where sure enough, below the crested waves the water swirls black with hints of silver.

Even though the water is far below, I reach down my hand to get sprayed. "I wonder what it would be like to dive into that."

I hear him chuckle behind me. He presses his hands against my arms. "I can help you with that, if you like."

I grab him. "I'll pull you in with me."

He laughs out loud and leans his elbows on the wood, the wind rippling his white blouse.

"It would be beautiful under there, that's for sure."

I nod and bring my arms down next to his, a fresh warm breeze from the wind pressing my dress against my body. "It would be so quiet and peaceful. Like a whole different world."

He chuckles. "I used to be terrified of the water."

I turn my head to him, my curls flopping to the other side by the wind. "You were?"

He nods, looking at the horizon. "I almost drowned when I was four. I was at the harbor with my father and slipped on the wet wood of the deck and fell in. It was a windy day, and the waves felt huge. I think I swallowed a gallon's worth of saltwater." He rumples his hair with his hand, grinning. "I was fine. Sailors pulled me out. I wasn't even hurt—just scared. It took me years to finally get over that fear."

"Funny how things like that stick with us for so long."

He turns to face me, leaning on one elbow on the railing. "So what was it like growing up as royalty? As the daughter of the king?"

I raise my eyebrows and cock my head. "Strict. There was always a pressure to live up to the standard of royalty and even more pressure for me being the heir. I didn't have a normal childhood. People didn't treat me normally." As another mist from the ocean settles on the deck, I taste salt on my tongue. "I don't know. It was like I was on a pedestal, and people wouldn't dare to reach up to me. I never felt like a real person—only a piece of royalty who couldn't get much more personal with people than eye contact." I roll down one of my dress's sleeve that had wrinkled in the wind. "I hated people acting like that with me. I felt normal, so when people treated me like I was different, I didn't like it. I couldn't go anywhere without an escort, and anytime I was in the village, people looked at me like I was another from another world or something." Turning my back on the water, I rest my hands on the railing and face the deck, where a few sailors carry out their night's work. "Eventually I think that started to change me. I began to feel the difference that people treated me with. And having everyone always pampering me and praising me—it confuses your view of life, making you think you're someone you're not." I look down and watch the wind ripple the bottom of my dress at my ankles.

He takes a step closer to me. "I think the life of royalty is harder than most people think it is." I feel his hand brush my neck. When I slowly turn to him, his blue eyes seem brighter than the moon. "Who would have known it would put you through all of this." His hand travels to my hair.

I think about his words. If I hadn't been born into my family, I wouldn't have experienced all that I had. I would have been completely different.

He takes my hand. "Let's go to the forecastle deck."

I smile and nod. He leads me across the deck and up the stairs.

Craning my neck to try to see as many stars as possible, I exhale. "I wonder what the sunrise would be like up here."

"Mmm." Still holding my hand, he looks up at the stars with me. "I imagine it would be breathtaking."

He points to a cluster in the sky. "Look! Doesn't that cluster of stars all look like one big star together?"

I look for a minute at the tiny lights, trying to find what he said. Then I see it. One big star, drawn by several little stars all aligned perfectly, as if made for that purpose.

He puts his arm around me and brings me in front of him, where I settle my back against his chest.

He breathes out. "I know there are many things I'll miss about the sea."

I smile.

———◄o►———

"Land ho!"

I need no less than two seconds to jump off my bed and rush up to the main deck.

Leaning over the railing, I search for the tiny dot that will be my first sight of my homeland. A black speck, as tiny as a pebble, climbs over the horizon. Aundria. I'm almost home.

"There it is. Home sweet home. You'll be there within a day."

Recognizing James's voice, I smile and continue staring at the horizon. "I can't wait," I whisper.

Memories stab my heart. The last time I was home, my mother was there. And my father was healthy, active, and strong.

James leans to peer at my face. "What are you thinking about?"

I bite a corner of my lip. "The last time I was home, my parents were there and healthy."

"Ah." He reaches out and places his hand on top of mine. "That makes two of us."

I intertwine my fingers with his, and then we both let go, aware of others around us.

My gaze plants on the faraway dot. Can I prepare myself for what my home country will now be like? And what of Alandar? Will King Maurice's death finally bring them peace? I ache beneath a sudden rush of compassion. "How are the people back in Alandar doing?"

"They're weak and struggling." He massages his chin. "All of them hated King Maurice but carried a deathly fear of him. Many Alandarin men were forced against their will to serve in his army." He flexes his jaw. "He compelled brother to fight against brother. No one could leave Alandar. Any who tried were executed, or if they were women and children, they were sold as slaves."

I stare into the water, my spine prickling.

"We now have Aundrian soldiers helping them," he continues. "Many of the Alandarins are without homes and separated from family. Some are also sick and wounded. Our soldiers are giving them homes, reuniting them with family, and caring for their needs. They're rebuilding and healing." He pauses for a minute. "They'll bring some Alandarins to Julinar and some to Aundria. We have strong leaders camped there."

Thoughts of Betsy and Martin capture my thoughts. Maybe, maybe …

"You'll be coming of age soon, won't you?"

His words cut into my thoughts. I nod. "Yes, in five weeks I will be eighteen."

"Eighteen." His voice quiets.

Clouds stretch over the horizon to my right, a blue line opening up into millions of waves. "Do you have any other family in Aundria?" I ask.

"No, I don't." His eyes cloud. "But I will remain at the castle under the direction of your father."

I turn back to the sea. He's alone in the world, with no one to look to for guidance or love. My thoughts wing to my father. Never before did I realize how blessed I am to have him by my side.

I lean my back against the railing. "Did you never have any siblings?"

He wipes his hands over the wood. "My mother miscarried three times. One of her babies survived but only for two weeks." He rubs his mouth. "It hurt our family greatly."

My dress flaps against my legs. I just look at him. We're both too familiar with the pain of loss.

"So now it's just me," he continues, giving me a sad smile.

Swallowing, I turn closer to him.

He reads my thoughts. "It's all right. A fellow's got to live with what he's got, right?"

But alone?

A sailor scoots a crate to the side with his foot as he approaches us. I groan inwardly.

"Your Highness, His Majesty desires your company," the sailor says.

I pull my eyes from James and twist toward the sailor. "Thank you, sir." With a last glance at James, I whisper, "I'll be back," and walk across the deck and into the dark of below.

"Lorelle!" my father exclaims from his bed when I enter. "I am pleased to see you."

"You sent for me, Father? Is everything all right? How are you feeling?"

He rumbles out a chuckle. "You're not worrying about me, are you?"

I work out a knot in my hair. "Yes, I am."

"You needn't be," he answers, his eyes twinkling and a grin pulling his lips. "Now come and sit beside me."

I settle myself on the bed.

"I've been thinking about you a great deal lately," he says.

My ears perk. His tone has changed.

"In about five weeks, you will step from a girl to a young woman."

As he pauses, I nod.

"And you will come to the point where you will need to make a change in your life." His gaze clutches me, suddenly intense and demanding. "I'm talking about marriage, Lorelle."

I jerk my head to the side. Something that feels like bile simmers in my stomach.

"I know you are aware of my friendship with King Lionel of Lonegalde," he continues.

I nod, thinking of the small country planted a sea away from Aundria.

"A month ago, his eldest son, Prince Garreth, turned twenty-four. We have for some time talked about the two of you. Of course, during the past few months the war has been at its extreme, so my mind has not fallen there. But now, Daughter, I think it is time."

My shoulders lock. I gulp as my mind twists into a war of confusion and rebellion.

"King Lionel and Queen Letha agree the marriage between you and Prince Garreth is the correct and proper act. After you come of age, we expect you to accept his hand."

I rub my hand up and down my arm. "Father, forgive me, but I do not even know Prince Garreth. I have met him only a few times in the past."

"Granted, but there is no law saying you have to have a personal relationship with your fiancé."

My throat squeezes. I bite my tongue, trying to swallow down objections. Looking into his eyes, I see it—slight hardness, coldness. And I know. The war has changed him.

"You will grow to love Prince Garreth, Lorelle. I know you have doubts, but you need to put them aside right now and trust me."

I force the bitter words out. "Yes, Father."

"The marriage will be held at the Aundrian palace. However, no word is to be said of this yet until we announce it." His face softens, and his warm smile resurfaces. "Prince Garreth is going to be blessed more than he realizes. He is about to wed one very beautiful, charming young woman."

I pinch out a smile, trying to use his compliments to shove away my protests.

"The King and Queen will be arriving with Prince Garreth in a couple of weeks. They will stay in the west wing of the palace until the day of your marriage." He rubs his thumb below his eye. "Beforehand, there will be a celebration held in your honor. The wedding will be held one month later. We will begin preparations immediately."

I stare at him. This is happening. This is actually happening.

"You are the destined queen of Aundria, Lorelle." He smooths his hand over his pillow. "People will look to you as their leader. In fact, they're already starting to."

I stand to my feet, idly smoothing my dress. "Thank you, Father. If you will excuse me, I think I will retreat to my bedroom and rest a while."

He nods. He reaches for my hand and kisses it. "I love you, my daughter."

"And I you, Father." I turn and hurry through the door. Once in my room, I flop on my bed. I still love my father, but now defiance against his wishes threatens me with a heat so intense I think my skin could boil.

Within two months, I will be the wife of Prince Garreth.

The shudder that shocks my spine catches my breath in my throat. I try to remember Prince Garreth's kind manners when we met in the past, but only faded memories float past me like gray clouds.

I stare at the ceiling and groan. Rolling over, I look out my window into the pure blue sky stretching over the sea.

"You are the destined queen of Aundria, Lorelle. People will look to you as their leader. In fact, they're already starting to." My mattress feels hard beneath me. Father is right—people's eyes will be on me. I am the daughter of the king of Aundria. People know me. They respect and honor me.

And right then and there, lying on my bed, I know I want to do something with my life. I want to be someone more than just a princess, more than just a piece of royalty who stands like a statue as people bow at her feet. I want to touch other people's lives, to serve those around me, to live my life to glorify and serve God.

Yet I think of a future as queen with a man beside me that I love and who loves me. Not a man I hardly know.

I cover my face with my hands. The sailors' shouts drift downward from up on the deck. Captain Carrington's voice calls for James.

The ship climbs a wave and then crashes down it. I clutch my stomach and curl into a ball. Something like a bitter juice fills the back of my throat. Funny. I haven't been seasick since my last voyage.

I sit up on my bed and walk to the door, trying to ignore the swirl in my gut. Sunlight from above streams down as I open the door and walk to the main deck.

The black dot still stands like an ant on the horizon. I can't even succeed in telling myself it's grown closer. I cross to the railing and curl my hands around the wood. My lips puff as another sigh rushes through them.

Marriage. The word crawls around in my head with claws for feet. I've always dreamed it would be romantic and beautiful. Witnessing the joy and trust between my parents always inspired me. I've dreamed of a relationship like theirs—strong, durable, and unwavering.

And they weren't forced together. Theirs was a relationship that formed freely, developed freely, and strengthened as the years continued. How can two people forced together for the rest of their lives develop a relationship like that?

Marriage. How the word has changed from a sweet melody to a threat!

I watch James talk with a sailor, his shirt rippling in the breeze. He curls his hands together at the back of his neck and nods as the sailor speaks. I run my hand through my hair and turn back to the railing.

Seconds later, James dodges another sailor carrying a large coil of rope and jogs up to me. "You're back! I've been waiting for you." He takes his place beside me and rests his hand upon mine for a quick second before he draws it away. I want to reach my fingers back to his—until a pain like a cluster of needles clogs my throat. I have a fiancé.

I pull my hand farther away from him and turn my back. "Excuse me, James—Sir Wellington—I ..."

I don't even want to try. I can feel his eyes burning into me. Before the silence explodes in my ears, I turn and rush away from him to the other side of the ship.

I steal my head around, searching for where I left him. He still stands beside the other railing, his eyes fixed on the place where I just was. Confusion and hurt mar his face. I tear my gaze away, my throat burning like crackling embers trapped beneath logs of wood.

Prince Garreth. An arranged marriage. I will now be tied to him, and no one else, for the rest of my life.

After years of not seeing each other, of not even knowing what the other was like, we are to get married. Married. Married.

My head pounds. I squeeze my eyes shut.

CHAPTER 18

Hours later, I slip into my father's cabin. Slivers of afternoon sun squeeze through the window's barely parted curtains as I cross over to the bed. Sitting down beside him, I smile, glad to see that the color has seeped back into his cheeks.

His lips form a grin. "Dear Lorelle, how are you doing this afternoon?"

"I'm all right, Father, thank you," I half lie. "How do you feel?"

He scowls under his breath and grips one corner of his blanket. "Well, I can tell you that I'm ready to get off of this bed. Lying here all day and all night, it's enough to make one go mad." He reaches for my hand and squeezes it. "But I have you here, and just seeing your beautiful face every day brings me great joy and comfort."

I smile and squeeze his hand back. "How's your leg?"

"It hurts." His eyes shimmer with genuine pain. "But I'll be fine."

An edge of his blanket compresses under my fingers as I rub it between my hands. "I can't stop worrying about you, Father. You—"

He gives a curt toss of his head. "Why should you worry about me? I'm recovering slowly but surely. The only thing that really aches now is my old back." His eyes twinkle with mirth. "So I am ordering you not to worry."

I grin at him and whisper, "Just please get better."

"My mind is already made up on that point. I just don't think my body has heard me yet."

His attempts at humor barely cover the fatigue and weariness still lurking in his eyes. "Father, have you thought any more on what I said to you a couple days back?"

He lays his head deeper into the pillow. "Oh, Lorelle, don't begin on that. Please."

I pause. With the pain my father experienced through the war, emotionally and physically, God must not seem the loving Savior to him as He does to me.

I try again. "God can heal your hurt, Father. He promises strength and comfort throughout any pain."

My father runs a hand through his hair as he leans his head back. "I've stayed one way all my life. I'm not about to convert now."

I tilt my head. "Why not?"

A twisted sigh rushes out. "Oh, Lorelle."

"Do you know where you're going when you die?"

He stops his hand in his hair. "I believe in purgatory."

"Why? What evidence do you have for that? You've only heard that from men. Mortal men."

His expression changes, darkening but tinted with curiosity. "What conclusion are you trying to reach?"

"God offers eternal life, Father, something that nothing else can give." I pause, fingering his blanket. "When I was in prison both times, I thought my world would fall apart, but He held it together."

Out of the corner of my eye, I see him tilt his head to the side.

"And he gave me such strength. He helped me endure every single day that stood before me." My lips pucker in a smile. "Oh, Father, I've never felt anything like that in my life. He gave me joy and never left my side, even when I was completely alone. All my life I carried bitterness toward King Maurice … for what he'd done"—I push away a flash of grief at the thought of Claire—"and what he was doing. Yet once I gave that to God, He gave me peace in return."

The walls change to a lighter brown as more sunlight struggles to break into the room. I stand up and walk to the window, pulling back the curtains further. More sunlight streams through, settling on the dust that lies sprinkled on the cabin's furniture. I continue, "I was always searching for something that would give me true contentment, but I never found it—that is, until I found Jesus." I pause, brushing my fingers over the window's glass. "Or rather, He found me."

The shouts of the sailors from up on deck fill the room's silence. Looking out at the waves as blue as a million topazes, the smooth fabric of my dress pressing on my back lets me know my father is staring at me. I turn around and meet his gaze.

Some of the lines have eased out of the skin on his face. Beneath knitted eyebrows, the sunlight brings out the flecks of gold in his eyes.

"Father?"

"You seem so genuine," he begins, "like a burden has been lifted off your shoulders. I've never seen you this way."

I sit on the bed and face him. "It's Him, Father. He's changed me."

He crumples an edge of the blanket in his fist. "I have no way of knowing this God will be any different. Almost everything that I have loved has left me. My wife and one of my daughters were ripped from me by the hands of murderers. My other daughter was imprisoned twice in a tyrant's dungeon. Dear friends of mine lost their lives battling for our country. My own kingdom and people were scarred severely. I barely made it out of this war alive."

He stops. The pain that etches onto his face sears me like fire. I reach for his hand and curl my fingers through his.

"The Bible says, 'He will never leave us nor forsake us.'"

His eyebrows furrow and he presses his lips together. "So you have devoted your life to Him?"

"Yes, I have. He died for me. What can I do but completely surrender my life to Him?"

I then tell him everything of Jesus' life, death, and resurrection. His eyes lock on mine and then flit to the dusty wooden floor below. Every moment of my imprisonment, of how God was there through it all, replays in my mind as I relay everything to him.

Though his forehead still wrinkles in thought, his brown eyes soften like a growing sunset. He sucks in a breath and releases it slowly. "How do I give my life to Him?"

I squeeze my hand on the blanket and inch closer to him on his sunlight-warmed bed. "Just ask Him to forgive you of your sins, and then commit your life to Him." The ship rolls over a wave, flooding the room in a soft blue hue and then melting back into the gold of the sun again. I bite my lip in a grin. "Ask Him to come into your heart."

------◄o►------

The excited shouts of the sailors filter down to my room. I blink my eyes open. Sunlight streaks in and bounces off the wooden walls, stinging my eyes like a giant pin. I roll over and bury my head deeper into the pillow. The cries continue.

A yawn almost splits my head in two as I sit up and crawl out of bed. I swing toward the door. Yes, I'm hearing cheering. Excitement drives the yells, and I've heard that excitement before.

I grab my dress to my chest. Are we near to pulling into port?

The cold fabric of my dress cools my skin as I scramble into my clothes. After running a brush through my hair, I hurry out of my room and up the stairs to the main deck.

A breath of sea air catches in my throat. I grin. Only a few feet of waves separate our ship from Aundria's harbor. The streets overflow with people, all cheering and waving. Sailors rush around the deck, preparing for the end of the voyage.

I race to the railing and lean over, soaking in everything I can of my homeland. Trees with headdresses of green dot the land like erect soldiers. Mountains shine over the Kingston village like silver jewels.

Yet my beautiful home, the castle where I spent my childhood, has been stripped of its beauty. Towers, walls, and gates are crushed and crumbling. In the village itself, huts struggle to stand amid destroyed walls and piles of wreck and ruin. Here and there, land surfaces black and bare.

The cheers of the people draw my attention from the wreckage. Their faces erupt in smiles of joy and pride, and their hands wave like raindrops that never hit the ground. Fists of victory plunge into the air about the black ground.

I press my lips together in a smile and raise my hand, my back tingling with goose bumps. I've returned to my homeland.

The ship slides into harbor. I grab the railing as it hits the dock. Turning back to the deck, I weave through excited sailors and rush downstairs into my father's bedchamber and halt next to his bed.

His sparkling eyes tell me he knows. "We're arrived, haven't we?"

I nod.

His eyebrows slope down as he gives me a sad smile. "How does it look to you?"

I cock my head and watch a seagull flap past the window. "It's different, but oh, Father, it's still beautiful. It's still our beautiful home."

He smiles and nods. I kneel down and wrap my arms around him, my cheek against his. Sweat bathes his neck and face, but I kiss him anyway.

Home also means marriage. I wince and draw away from my father.

"Tell me what's on your mind."

I grimace. Father can always see my emotions, sometimes before I can even see them myself. Yet I can't let him see what fights within me now. I can't let my burden be added to his.

I force a tight smile. "I was just wondering where I will live after I am married." The words sting my tongue. I have a feeling I already know the answer.

His eyes darken. I stare harder as I realize it isn't the scolding look that simmered in his eyes the day before. It's … sorrow.

"You will live in Lonegalde with Prince Garreth."

I look down at my closed hands. Deep inside I hoped actually asking the question would make the answer different.

My father interrupts my thoughts, saying, "Ah, it will feel good to be home." He fumbles his fingers around the edge of his blanket. "And have you home with me."

We both turn to his window as the sound of barrels rolling down the gangplank joins the sailor's shouts above.

His cold fingers slip into mine. I look down to see his brown eyes looking up at me. "You go, my daughter. I'll join you shortly."

My hand tightens around his. "Are you sure?"

He nods and motions me forward. I lean down, and he plants a kiss on my forehead.

A cloud has slipped over the sun when I step back onto the deck. Captain Carrington rounds the corner the same moment as I. A quick step to the side saves me from ramming into his chest. Even though his eyes harden with focus, he smiles at me. "Your Highness, a pleasure to see you again."

I pull out a smile.

He motions toward the deck. "A carriage is waiting beside the ship, ready to take you to the palace. Knights will escort you. Are you ready to depart now?"

"I am, thank you."

"Then excuse me for one moment."

He darts through sailors to where James is working. James stops helping with cargo and delivers Captain Carrington his attention. The captain talks for a minute, gestures to me, and then pats him on the shoulder, sending him over. I try to avert my gaze and pin it to the ship's floor, but too late, I meet his eyes for a second that passes too quickly.

"Your Highness." Out of the corner of my eye, I notice him lower himself in a bow. "Allow me to escort you to the palace." He extends his arm. I accept it, unconsciously wrapping my hand around his wrist as the urge to run and hide with him and tell him everything steals my breath. He turns and looks at me.

A sailor bumps into the James's shoulder. The sailor gives a quick nod of apology and hurries to the gangplank. James follows. I press my lips together, having no idea where to look as he leads me through the mass of sailors and down the gangplank.

Yet when I step foot onto Aundrian ground, for a moment I forget about everything.

I am home.

CHAPTER 19

James—Sir Wellington, I remind myself—stops beside a carriage near the dock. The gold trimming and satin draping bring back a flood of memories. A footman opens the door and lowers his head.

I release my grip on Sir Wellington's arm. He offers his hand, and I grasp it, but before I can mount, I find myself staring into his vibrant blue eyes. His gaze holds onto mine, his fingers warm beneath my own, and for a minute I'm tempted to tell him everything, right then and there.

The cries and cheering of the Aundrians jerk me back. I turn and rush inside. Once the door shuts behind me, I sink into the cushions and stare across at the other plush bench. I never expected to be so upset as this over a marriage. Oh, how that word now sounds like danger to my very life.

When the carriage lurches and rolls across the road, I position myself by the window. Every Aundrian's eyes are on me. I reach out and begin my traditional wave, forcing a smile to surface.

My grin soon climbs from pasted to genuine. In the distance, a church steeple pinpoints the sky. The wind pushes against my hand as I pause midair for a second. He's been here the whole time, and I haven't paid any attention to Him. I haven't thanked Him for carrying me home safely. As I feel His peace wash over me now, I know He is still carrying me.

We soon leave the village behind us, and the beautiful Aundrian palace is almost at my fingertips. I poke my head out the window.

The carriage rocks to a stop, and I sit back as the footmen opens the door. Again, Sir Wellington waits, his hand extended to help me exit. I try to ignore the way my chest tingles when my fingers touch his.

The huge gates surrounding the palace yard swing open, and Sir Wellington offers his arm. We walk through the entrance and across the yard to the palace doors. My time away from home suddenly shrinks to what feels like only a day, yet at the same time, I feel as if it's been years since I've touched these palace walls.

Before we enter, Sir Wellington ducks his head to whisper in my ear, "Your Highness, may I be so bold as to ask if I have offended you in any way? You are not as you have been."

He's right. Nothing in my life is as it was. Everything, from my family to my home, has changed. I've changed.

"I'm sorry," I finally whisper, looking at a cluster of trees.

He doesn't move. "What happened, Lorelle? Have I done something to anger you?"

At this I shoot my head back around. "Oh, no! No, not at all. I just … I mean … no. No."

He sets his jaw in a firm line, his eyes searching mine. "You haven't acted like this before. At least, not since you changed."

I wrap my arms around myself, cocking my head. "Ja— Sir Wellington, please. Something has arisen that I do not have the freedom to discuss."

His gaze still holds me, studying me. The wind pulls his blond hair over his forehead. "After all these months, I thought you would be excited to be home."

"Oh, I am. It's just that—"

I stop. His eyes question me with such intensity and concern my hair stands on end. My thoughts travel back to all the times he proved his trustworthy character. Surely, now, he deserves the truth.

151

I grip the sides of my dress. After staring at the marble below us, I raise my eyes to his. "I'm engaged."

The look that covers his face almost frightens me. Sorrow, disappointment, almost anger. He looks defeated. He swipes his hand over the back of his neck. "To whom?"

"Prince Garreth of Lonegalde." I press my fingers against my palm. "His parents and my own have been planning our marriage for years. I only a day ago discovered that."

Seconds pass before he speaks again. "So it is this engagement that has been causing you to feel so miserable?"

He is able to read me so well. I nod.

He turns from me, his eyes scanning the sky. The rigid set of his shoulders and flex of his jaw needles my stomach.

When he turns back to me, the hard edges in his face have softened, but sorrow still huddles in his eyes like empty shadows. "Let me wish you a joyful and successful marriage." He clasps my hand and kisses it, his lips hesitating before he draws away. When he brings his head back up, the crease above his eyes and the lingering way he looks at me tells me he wants to say more, but all he finishes with is "Prince Garreth is about to be blessed beyond his years. God be with you, Your Highness." After an all-too-short second, he reluctantly releases my hand and lowers himself in a bow. He then walks across the yard, passing the soldiers and lords who are making their way toward me.

I stand there, feeling deflated. Funny, how his compliment was the same as my father's.

The lords and knights reach me and lead me inside. I swallow and nod to them. When I step foot inside my home, instead of the expected urge of excitement, a relieving kind of exhaustion showers through my body.

Thank You, Lord. Thank You.

If it is possible to squeeze God's hands so hard His knuckles turned white, then I am doing just that.

One of the lords offers his arm. "May I escort you to your bedchamber?"

"You may." I loop my arm through his.

As we walk, I look around and let out a long imprisoned sigh. Though decorations and furniture are missing, the castle still emits the Aundrian pride.

Once alone inside my bedroom, I shut the door and walk through the room, step by step, memory by memory. I sweep my finger through some dust on my bedside table.

Walking to my window, faint sunlight breaking through the clouds warms my body. Groups of men scattered over the village rebuild homes and shops, while others load piles of broken bricks and snapped wood onto wagons to be taken away.

I wrap my arms around myself. The Aundria I used to know will never be mine again. Memories from my childhood, when I was a free girl and enjoying life with my mother and father in a country strong on its feet, gather in my mind. I will never be that girl again.

CHAPTER 20

A warm afternoon breeze swirls around me, carrying the salty scent of the sea. I look up from my book and close my eyes. I have two hours to myself. Two precious hours before the man who will become my future arrives.

The sound of galloping horses cuts into my thoughts. I turn to look, my attendants all looking in the same direction. A group of men on horses trot toward us. The bows, arrows, and swords complete the party. They must be returning from hunting.

The four horses stop beside us. As the leader lowers his head, I recognize him as one of my father's lords and top advisors, Lord William Conway. The other two I do not know, but the fourth is Sir Wellington. I press my book between my hands.

Lord Conway tips his head. "Your Highness, it is a fine day to be out of doors reading."

I squeeze out a smile. "It is just that, Lord Conway." His chestnut-colored hair ripples and his green eyes shine. "And a fine day to be hunting, as well." My eyes dart from Sir Wellington and back to Lord Conway before I can help myself. His blue eyes are fixed on me. I shake my head. "Did you have much success?"

"Unfortunately, not much," he answers. "This was our last trip of the summer. Tomorrow, two of these young men are heading to sea."

I shift my gaze to the three other rides then quickly return it the leader. "Who?"

He motions to a red-haired one. "Sir Alexander Cunnings"—
Lord Conway cuts his hand through his hair—"and Sir James
Wellington."

I grip my book, hard. Leaving for the sea? "To where, my lord?"

"The island of Gadelin," he answers. "We've made an
agreement with the foreigners living there concerning the small
island's plentiful sources. It is rich with extraordinary fruit."

"I see." I steal a glance at Sir Wellington. His horse ripples his
mane as Sir Wellington adjusts the bridle.

A squirrel jumps from one branch to another above us,
rustling some leaves. I turn back to the lord. "Who is the captain
of the ship, may I ask?"

"Captain Carrington."

"Ah, a fine man indeed. He will be an excellent leader for the
voyage."

"I couldn't agree with you more." He situates his reins in his
hands. "Now if you will excuse us, Your Highness, we will be on
our way. It was a pleasure seeing you."

He bows his head as I nod. "Good day, Lord Conway."

"Good day, Princess."

As the men kick their heels into the horses' sides, I look at
James one last time. His horse eases into a trot, but before he
rides past me, I quickly breathe in as I catch it—a nod, ever so
slight and gentle.

The second passes, and they're gone. I bite my lip as a cardinal
flies down to a branch, bright red against the green leaves. The
past few days I've kept thinking about him, without wanting to
and without meaning to. And now, he's heading to sea? For how
long?

I shake my head. It doesn't matter.

———◄○►———

Just as the final pin is pushed into my hair, the cheering
explodes. I move from my maid's grasp and look toward the
window. They've arrived.

155

A ship matching Aundria's in size and opulence declares itself as the newest member of the harbor. I watch sailors trudge off the gangplank, loaded down with chests. Soldier after soldier line the ship as a man and woman step from below deck into the open air, bedecked in jewelry, fringe, and silk. My future parents-in-law.

I turn from the view and just reach my door when a knock sounds. The maid twists the knob and pulls it open.

"They have arrived, Your Highness," a servant says, his hand extended toward mine. I slip my fingers through his and turn to walk to the stairs.

Our steps carry the familiar echo between the marble walls. We reach the bottom and walk to the reception hall. I remember playing years ago in the then-empty room, hiding under the chair-lined table stretched across the floor. I used to love brushing my hands over the velvet draperies that hung from the ceiling. The candles have always sparkled like stars in my mind.

The servant leads me to the royalty table on a platform at the front of the room, and I sit in the chair. The doors swing wide to usher in my father and a group of servants helping him to his chair.

My lips stretch in a proud grin. His gold crown perches on his graying hair, and his red-and-gold robe flows behind him like a waterfall. When he looks at me, a small smile gives his cheeks a warm glow. Somehow his thin face doesn't look so thin today.

It takes only a few minutes for my nerves to suck what feels like everything out of my stomach, making it hollow. A train of knights enter, and as I wrap my hands together, I hear the words, "Their Majesties, the king and queen of Lonegalde, and His Royal Highness, Prince Garreth."

The servants help my father to his feet as I rise to mine. The great doors open wider as the procession enters. Servants, maids, dukes, and lords, headed by the royalty themselves, stride to the front of the room.

And that is when I see my future husband. Green eyes peer from beneath thick, wavy, brown hair as the prince bows.

"Welcome, King Lionel, Queen Letha, Prince Garreth!" my father says. "Welcome to Aundria. We are honored that you have come."

As they lower themselves again, my father and I bow and curtsy with them.

"You remember my daughter, Her Royal Highness, Princess Lorelle." My father gestures to me, and I look at the king and queen. The queen's hazelnut-shaped eyes are the purest green I have ever seen, almost like an aqua green. Her sharply trimmed eyebrows and firm jaw harden her appearance.

My father waves his hands in the air. "Please, be seated."

They mount the platform to the table where the servants pull out chairs for them. My heart picks up speed as Prince Garreth is seated beside me. His red-and-gold vest, matched with a snow-white satin blouse, plays with the light. Out of the corner of my eye I see him look at me.

Well, I will have to do the same sooner or later. I turn to look at him.

His lips are stretched in a grin, accompanied by two dimples. Green eyes with flecks of brown smile at me as he gives me a quick nod.

"Good evening, Your Highness. It is a pleasure and honor to see you again."

"And you."

"It's been a long time."

"Yes, it has been."

One side of his mouth rises in a lopsided grin. "I'm sure we've both changed quite a bit." He scratches his temple. "How many years ago was that … eleven? Twelve?"

"I think it's been twelve," I answer.

He shakes his head. "Time does fly. How have you been?"

My stomach begins to feel full again, not hollow as it had minutes ago. "I've been well, thank you. And you?"

He tilts his head in thought. "Every day now is preparing for the day I will become king. I'm sure you know what that is like."

I chuckle and nod.

157

He chuckles with me and then leans forward to whisper, "Nerve-racking, isn't it?"

I shoot an anxious glance at the other guests seated at the table. For the moment, they chat with my father and pay us no mind. I turn back to him. "It is! Very … surreal."

"I couldn't agree more. You always think that time is so far away, and then suddenly it's looming ahead of you."

I brush my hands together. "I know exactly what you mean. It's fast but, in a way, exciting."

He nods in agreement. "It's energizing, even … empowering." He stops for a minute and then looks down as he laughs. "I didn't mean that literally."

I laugh with him. "I understood what you meant."

He turns more toward me, his green eyes bright. "I'm sure you must be grateful the war has ended. I hope it didn't hurt you too much."

He probably has no idea what has happened to me, but why would I tell him?

I give him a small smile. "I survived it. God was faithful."

He smiles back. "I'm glad to hear that. I'm sorry it was such a long and difficult time. I cannot imagine what you went through."

"Thank you," I answer, settling my hands in my lap. "I am truly grateful it is over. I hope nothing like that ever happens again, especially because any war that arises in the future will be held in my hands as queen."

He rests his wrists on the table. "I am sure together we will be able to stand strong if anything does arise."

My stomach twists. This is the first time he's mentioned *us*. What did he think as he said it? Is he indifferent or, like me, hating the idea but knowing we have no other choice?

Feminine laughter rings in the air, and a chair rumbles over wood as a person shifts his position. I almost jump, remembering we aren't the only two people in the room. Scanning the space, I wonder if I will catch any uninvited glances, but people only nod in conversation.

"How long have you known?" he asks.

I swing my head back around. It takes me a few seconds to realize what he is asking me. "My father told me a few weeks ago."

He rubs the back of his neck. "It was only a few months ago my parents told me."

Silence pushes in between us. I stare for a minute at the delicate linen stretched over the table and then finally look at him.

We both smile and chuckle the awkwardness away, and then he says, "I did feel surprise."

I blow out a breath. "I know I did."

"They told me they had been planning this since our infancy. I had no idea."

"I hadn't either."

He runs his hand along the tablecloth. "You always hear of it happening to other people, but when it happens to you ..." He looks at me again and gives me an apologetic smile. "I'm sorry if it crushed any personal hopes you had for your own future."

I almost start at the thought. Did it?

I squeeze my hands together in my lap. "Thank you. I'm sorry too if that was the case with you. I truly am."

A sigh puffs out his cheeks and lips, and I find myself doing the same. We both begin laughing, despite the curious glances charged at us.

"Thank goodness," he says. A smile, full and genuine, spreads across his face. "Thank goodness."

I smile with him.

The meal ends with a favorite from my childhood—rich lemon pudding drizzled with sweet cream. After King Lionel, Queen Letha, and the rest of the royal parties pay their formal congratulations to Prince Garreth and I, we leave the table to begin the dances. Each lord has a lady on his arm, each duke has a duchess, and soldiers, servants, and maids accompany us on our walk to the ballroom.

I swallow back any nerves. The dancing will be fine.

The massive ballroom shines with gold-painted walls, rich wood floors, and intricate paintings on the ceiling. Huge sconces line the room, their candles sparkling like life-size jewels. A chandelier hangs from the center of the ceiling, draped with hundreds of strings of diamonds. Red drapery, adorned with gold fringes, hangs from a balcony that wraps around the entire room. Tables with more desserts and drinks dot the walls.

Prince Garreth inhales sharply. "This is breathtaking." He breathes out as we step into the room. "How beautiful."

I smile. It's been years since I've been in this room. Little did I know on the last day I was here that the next time I would step into this room, I would be on the arm of my fiancé.

People file into the room. As the musicians ready themselves in their chairs on the balcony, Prince Garreth looks at me and smiles. "Can I get you a refreshment while we wait for the dances to begin?"

I'm not thirsty or hungry, but it gives us something to do. "Yes, that would be lovely. Thank you."

He leads me to one of the refreshment tables, covered with multiple bowls of punch and bottles of champagne and other wines.

He lifts a glass. "Champagne?"

"Yes, thank you."

A servant pours a glass for me, and then the prince places it in my hand. After the servant serves him a glass, he lifts it in the air. "To our love life."

My stomach recoils. I stare at him as he swallows back two gulps and then grins at me. I set my glass on the table.

The steady hum of the instruments signal the beginning of the first dance. He offers his arm again, and this time even the rippling muscle underneath his satin sleeve doesn't distract me from my building uncertainty.

We line up with the other couples in the center of the room. The dance master of the evening calls the first dance, and the music begins.

We step towards each other. His green eyes lock onto mine. Back, forward, to the side, behind. Our hands touch. His larger fingers intertwine with each of mine. He pulls me closer, holding my gaze. His hand slides around my waist, followed by his arm. Sidestep, back, spin, together. He twirls me under his arm in time to the music and then pulls me close to him again. His breath heats my neck.

I break our gaze. We turn away from each other, dance a few steps with a different person, and then come back together again. When I look back, his eyes aren't looking into mine. I follow them downward to the neckline of my dress. Heat flares in my cheeks. I pull away from him and turn with the music, gritting my teeth. He's a good six inches taller than me.

When the music brings us back together, I let our hands be the only things that touch. But as the dance calls for, he wraps me in his arms and then twirls me out again. He then turns me under into his embrace, and we follow the steps with the other couples.

Minutes pass. If anyone is an actor, he is. Anger churns in my gut, followed by disappointment. During dinner, I dared to hope.

We step apart, step together, and he brings his head close to mine. I duck and twirl with the music, my heart beating ...

And the dance is over.

The couples bow to each other, and he walks toward me with his hand outstretched. I have to take it. He leads me back to the table where our champagne glasses still wait. After handing me mine, he takes a sip of his, looks at me, and grins. "Now I know what I have to look forward to."

My neck tenses. Heat crawls up my neck like a swarm of ants. I turn my head to look anywhere other than his face.

Couples talking and laughing, glasses of wine in their hands, scatter around the ballroom. Ladies' dresses fan out like wings, rich and dripping with grandeur. Men's vests shine like flames. I look through the sweeping fabric and sparkling jewels and see two eyes brighter than sapphires matched with blond hair. James. Looking at him, my stomach twists into a knot. Yet as I look, I don't see frustration from him. I see only support. Our gazes hold frozen in the air, suspended over the room. My mind swims, waves of memories and emotions plunging over a surface so still in my mind I can hear the beating of my heart.

Cold, icy fingers slip into my hand, snapping my head back. I stare into the green eyes of Prince Garreth and look down at his hand in mine. I pull it away from him. "Please control yourself from physical touch, Prince Garreth."

His eyes spark with surprise and mockery. "Don't try to avoid the inevitable, Princess Lorelle. After all, this is a life-ordained match, is it not?"

I calmly set my glass down and turn to face him. "No, Prince Garreth, it is not. This is just arranged from the lips and actions of our parents."

He cocks his head at me, a wry smile thinning his lips. A shudder races up my spine. I can see his warm demeanor sizzling away into nothing.

He offers his hand. "Shall we join the waltz?"

I look to the dance floor, where a number of couples sway to the music. My stomach swirls.

"Your Highness?" Lord Harmon steps to the side to let a couple pass.

"Lord Harmon!" I exclaim, thanking God for the distraction.

He kisses my hand. "Are you enjoying the evening?"

I angle away from Prince Garreth and his uncomfortable gaze. "I am, thank you."

Lord Harmon briefly congratulated me in the dining hall earlier, but this is the first time we have spoken in many, many weeks. I've missed his shining eyes and warm smile. I've missed the way I feel so comfortable and secure around him.

I give him a warm smile "I hope you have been doing well."

He pulls on his vest. "I have, thank you. The war has been occupying much of my time, but the Lord is good."

He holds my gaze for a moment. His steady dependability on that very first day away from home, when the war had freshly injected its poison into my body, strengthened and comforted me. God knew I needed him. How is it that before anything even happened, He orchestrated each person to come into my life at the exact right time to guide and protect me?

Lord Harmon breaks into my thoughts with a touch to my elbow. "I am so grateful you are now safe, Princess. You were constantly in my prayers."

My smile grows. "And I felt them, Lord Harmon. Thank you so much."

He gently pats my arm. Normally, an act like that would be considered improper and bold. But I don't care. I know limits can't stop everything.

The folds of my dress sway against my hand as somebody walks past. "Are you here at the estate for long?"

"I leave again tomorrow. I will be traveling to Chanstin, but it is not a long trip."

Ah, yes, the village on the east side of Julinar. I have heard of it but have never traveled there. "I wish you luck."

"Thank you, Princess."

A grunt grumbles in the air. I turn my head to where Prince Garreth stands next to me. Has he been present the whole time?

"Ah, Prince Garreth," Lord Harmon says. "I hope you are enjoying your evening."

"I am, sir, thank you," he replies, sliding his eyes to me. "I was hoping I could convince this young lady to return to the dance floor with me." His hands wrap around my arm and he settles it in his. "Princess?"

Lord Harmon's gaze shifts from Prince Garreth to me. The encouragement that I find there eases my discomfort a little. He reaches out and gives my hand a quick squeeze before Prince Garreth spins me away.

The night drudges by with dance after dance. I twirl under his finger, my heart beating in my throat like a drum. How long can this last?

Eight dances later, I still haven't found my answer.

I pull back in Prince Garreth's arms, my feet following the dance's steps without thought. When we turn back in, a grin spreads across his face, pulling his lips taut.

"You are beautiful."

I keep my shoulders back. "Thank you, Prince Garreth."

"My parents certainly knew best when they chose you for me."

"We were chosen for each other."

We step away and then back again. "True, but my parents were aware of how important a beautiful wife would be for my position."

I pin his gaze. "Your position?"

"Surely the king of Lonegalde cannot be expected to have an unsightly wife for his queen." He licks his lips. "But that worry is now gone. I will have you all to myself."

The dance pulls us apart. Anger and humiliation clumps in my throat. My heart races with such energy that my breath feels sucked away from me.

He curls his arm tighter around my waist and pulls me in. I inhale sharply. Other dancing couples are in synchronization with us but are not as close as we are. Heat washes up my back. Gritting my teeth, I spin out of his grip as the dance ends with a musical blast.

The light and noise of the room suffocates me. I rush away from him, not caring if I didn't properly curtsey or if the nobility sees me leaving so abruptly the man I am to marry.

My hands clutching my dress, I brush past skirts, forcing myself not to run. Golden light from the candles and sconces blur past me as I reach one of the ballroom's doors, pull it open, and hurry inside, shutting it firmly behind me.

I've entered a small room, housing only a staircase. A silver glow shines from a balcony at the top of the winding staircase. I pick up my skirts and run up the steps, not stopping until I reach the top.

Cool air washes over my body. A white marble balcony gleams in the moonlight. Beyond it, the trees and leaves of the forest surrounding the castle sway with the breeze, rustling and creaking. I walk to the railing and wrap my hands around the cold surface. The nip of the air soothes the heat from my body, a beautiful contrast from the stifling heat of the ballroom.

Lifting my head to the sky, I blink. Millions of stars sparkle like diamonds, twinkling and laughing. If only I could join them.

A sound on the steps jerks me around. Has a soldier been sent to retrieve me?

I face the entrance, waiting. A black form switches to a man's figure as he climbs closer to the moonlight. James steps onto the balcony.

I fumble my hand in the folds of my skirt. "What are you doing up here?"

"I followed you. I saw the finish of the dance and watched you steal away."

I turn back to the quiet of the forest.

"Are you all right?" he asks.

I shake my head. "Please go. If someone finds us up here ..."

"Then I should say farewell. I'm leaving early in the morning."

I swallow. "How long will you be gone?"

"It depends. Weeks. Months. I don't know."

His booted steps scrape across the balcony. Out of the corner of my eye I see him stop beside me, his hands gripping the railing.

"I'm so sorry about tonight. If there was anything I could do ..."

Regret fills my throat. There is nothing anyone can do.

"Will you leave for Lonegalde?" he asks.

The question stings. Is this the last time I will see him—ever? "Yes."

I turn to him and speak before the urge welling inside me can be killed. "I wanted to thank you for all you've done the past few months. I was away from home and without family, and you not only cared for me, you risked your life for me." I swallow rising tears and lower my voice to a whisper. "I thank you with all of my heart."

He presses his lips together, lowering his lashes. "It was truly an honor, Your Highness."

"Allow me to wish you a pleasant and successful voyage." My cheek cries in protest as I bite it, hard.

"And I you, with your future."

I turn back to the forest, gripping the railing. Hurt lurches inside me. The truth falls out in half-whispers. "I can't. I can't marry someone I don't love. I can't."

Silence envelops the air.

"I can do all things through Christ who strengthens me."

His quiet words slow the beating of my heart. Yet, how can I? I turn and look at him, my eyes blurring.

"God will provide. He holds your future in His hands."

"How can a marriage that is forced into existence with an unwilling victim succeed?" I pause. "Were your parents forced to marry against their will?"

He gives a slow shake of his head. "No, they were not."

I rub my forehead. Worry and uncertainty have consumed so much of my thoughts that it is only now I feel the cold fear chilling my blood. "I cannot sacrifice myself to someone I hardly know and don't love."

His eyes well with deep understanding and pain. "God will hold your hand and guide you every step of the way. 'He will never leave thee nor forsake thee.'"

My head droops, feeling like a boulder on my shoulders. All of a sudden he is the only person in the world I can confide in. The only one who understands and the only one I can trust. "James, he's everything I didn't expect. He's awful. Marrying him will be torment, but I know there's no way out. And if my father sees my suffering, it will only hurt him. If I tell him, it will be worse, knowing I have pulled him into this struggle with me." I bite my lip. "I know I'm alone."

He clasps my hands tight, gripping them so hard I'm certain the blood drains from my fingers. "You're not alone. I'm here for you. I'm here for you always."

He stops, and I stare at him, holding my breath.

He looks down, and then brings his eyes back to mine. "No matter what happens, I will be here for you."

I swallow down a lump in my throat and lean my head against his chest as he lets go of my hands and wraps his arms around my shoulders, pulling me close.

"Don't ever forget that." His voice shakes as the words come out. I cling to him, the man who saved my life, who risked himself for me, who changed me.

"I'm sorry," I suddenly whisper. "I'm sorry this had to happen."

He holds me tighter, pressing his lips to my head. I just stand there, protected in his arms, my cheek against his chest. Here, if only for a few moments, I feel safe.

"I will never forget you, Lorelle."

I shut my eyes and press my cheek closer to his chest.

"I will never forget you," he repeats.

Standing there, secure in his embrace, knowing that the minute this ends I may never see him again, I am certain I will never forget him either.

CHAPTER 21

"Prop up my pillow, will you?" My father wiggles his shoulders.

I grasp my father's pillow and pull it upward. He settles into it and sighs with contentment. "It's been almost five weeks, Lorelle. How does it feel to be home?"

I sit on his bed. "Wonderful. You really never know how much a place means to you until you are forced to part from it."

"Very true." His warm smile lights his face like a ray of sun hitting an ocean wave. "It is different, though. Many loved ones are gone."

I stroke his blanket. "It feels emptier, doesn't it?"

His eyes deepen with remembering and longing. "Emptier. Quieter. Lonelier." He squeezes my hand. "That's why I'm glad I have you."

The bed creaks as I lean forward and kiss his rough, sweaty cheek. "The ship from Julinar will arrive tomorrow, won't it?"

"It will," he answers. "And an Alandarin ship a week or so after that. We are all very eager."

I continue to finger his bedspread, pondering. "Father, a few weeks back, before King Maurice was killed, did two Julinarin ships reach here?"

He frowns. "No, but we heard of their voyages. Alandarin ships attacked and sunk them."

I pinch some of the fabric, shocked. "I had no idea. That explains why we never heard from you."

He doubles over as he suddenly begins violently coughing. The bed beneath him trembles as his body revolts.

"Father!" I push my arms under his shoulders and support his heaving body, desperately trying to hush him, but the cough only rises in intensity. "Steady, Father, steady. Easy now."

His body, wet with sweat, fights against my grip. I hold firm, one hand on his head and one on his back. When he begins to calm down, relief washes over me.

"There, Father—"

A hunk of blood hurls out of his mouth, followed by silence. He falls into my hands, limp and white, his eyes wrinkled closed.

My heart pushes at my throat. I race out of the bedroom and down a long hallway, my feet unable to carry me fast enough. When I reach Doctor Adams's door, I pound my fists against it.

It swings open. "Your Highness! Is something wrong?" Doctor Adams studies my face, shock covering his. "Heaven help me. Your father?"

I nod. "He was coughing … There was blood …"

The doctor is already running past me, headed for the bedchamber. He thrusts open the door and rushes inside, myself not far behind.

As the man presses his hands over my father's chest, my father's shoulders sag. His gray and motionless body lies limp beneath sweat-soaked blankets.

Please, God. Please …

I sink into a chair, watching the doctor work. My father seemed fine just minutes ago … What happened? I gulp, my eyes never straying from the thin, gray face—the face that is fading away from me with each passing breath.

———◀O▶———

"He never fully recovered from his injury, Your Highness. Plus, there is age to consider. A man of sixty-seven shouldn't be under such strain."

I rub my neck, my nails scraping my skin, the other hand flattened against my chest. Afternoon sunlight streams through the sitting room's window and gathers a pool of sweat on my back.

"Right now he's sleeping," the doctor continues, running a weary hand through his hair. "His body is trying to fight off the damage from the blows he received in battle. Yet as weak as his condition is making him now, he is not succeeding very well."

Dread flickers to life in my chest as I sense what the doctor is trying to tell me.

He pulls his vest tighter around his chest. "I will come out and tell you: I am worried. His leg isn't healing in the way it should, and as I investigated more, I found internal damage done to his chest. That is what caused his coughing episode."

I dig my nails into my skin. Why did he not discover that before? "What caused his chest damage?"

"He was sneaking through a hallway, intending to rescue someone from the Alandarin dungeon. The ceiling above him collapsed, along with the walls all around him. While trying to escape, the stones crushed him."

The puzzle pieces slip together.

"I'll continue doing everything I can." He lowers himself in a bow. "I will return to his bedchamber now. Please excuse me." He turns and leaves the room, the door's closing echoing in the silence around me.

———◀◦▶———

Hours later, the last final rays of evening sun cast glittering patterns through the hallway as I hurry to my father's bedchamber. Outside his door, I tap quietly and then let myself in.

He sags against his pillows. The color and liveliness has been ripped from his body. His thin eyelids are sealed shut, his mouth set in a hard line.

I creep toward his side. He looks so exhausted ... so discouraged. Kneeling, I gently lace my fingers through his. "Father?"

His eyelids drag open. "Lorelle." A weak smile succeeds only at pulling the corners of his mouth.

"Oh, Father." I force a smile. "How do you feel?"

"Well, I—" He halts and groans. "M-My chest hurts. Oh! It feels like it's ... tightening."

I place my fingers lightly against his shoulder. "All of it?"

"No, just the middle," he answers, his voice quivering.

His chest rises and falls in heavy, short breaths. He seems to be struggling just to inhale.

"And my arm ... Oh, my arm hurts!"

This scares me. My father is not one to complain. The pain he is feeling now must be close to unbearable.

"Father—"

The door opens. Doctor Adams steps inside, a small, black bag in his hand.

"Your Highness, how is he?"

"He's complaining of intense pain," I answer, never more glad to see anyone in my life.

The doctor crosses to the bed, calm and steady. "Where, Your Majesty? Where is the pain?"

"My chest. And my arm."

"Which one?"

"My left."

Doctor Adams pulls back the bedcovers and gently presses his hands on my father's chest. "And what exactly does the pain feel like? Is it aching, tight, sharp ...?"

"It's ... tight," my father fumbles. "It feels like someone is squeezing me in a vice."

The alarm that leaps into the doctor's eyes shoots quivers down my spine. "Your Majesty, listen to me. Try to steady your breathing. I need to go fetch something to relax your muscles, but I will be back in minutes. Keep your breathing even and level until then."

After directing me with a cautioning glance, he turns and rushes out of the room. I turn my gaze from following him to my father's pale face and gently lay my hand on top of his. "That's right, Father. Steady your breathing. There now."

He stares at me through slitted eyelids. "Oh, Lorelle. You're so—beautiful, inside and out. Thank you for what you did for me. For sharing God's message of eternal life."

I squeeze his hand.

A faint smile appears on his face. "God has blessed me—beyond what I could ever deserve. He gave me a caring, loving daughter to strengthen and love me. I don't know ... how to thank Him. You'll be eighteen tomorrow, and you're g-growing into a beautiful young—woman. H-Happy birthday."

I bring his hand to my face, pressing my lips so hard against it they throb against my teeth.

The doctor races back into the room, another black bag in his hand. "Off the bed, please, Your Highness. Off the bed."

I hurry off but don't let go of his hand until I can't reach him anymore.

"Your Highness, would you be so kind as to leave the room for a few minutes?"

Alarm fills the doctor's eyes, but it's also mingled with pleading. I nod. A voice stops me at the door.

"I love you, Lorelle."

I turn around, tears pooling in my eyes. "I love you, Father."

A small smile, pained but so full of love, lights his face.

After one last look into his eyes, I turn and leave the room.

The door's click echoes in the hallway.

CHAPTER 22

"Your Highness." Firm knocking jerks me awake.

I jump out of bed and swing the door open, my skin cool beneath just my nightdress.

A maid stands in the doorway. "Doctor Adams has requested your presence in your father's bedchamber."

Oh no. I snatch my silk robe from my wardrobe and throw it over my shoulders as I run down the stairs with the maid. Nearing my father's bedchamber, a servant opens the door and slips out, hurrying down a back hallway. When I reach the door, I raise my fist and knock, dread churning like a hurricane inside me.

It opens, revealing an energy-sapped Doctor Adams.

I try to see past him. "My father?"

He drags his eyes to me and opens his mouth to speak but emits nothing.

I begin to push past him, but he catches my arm and holds me. "Please, Your Highness. Your father ..."

Bells toll in the air.

I stare at the wall. My breath sucks out of me as my body numbs over with cold.

The words *heart attack* and *failure* and *minutes ago* drift over my head. No, no ...

"He has passed, Your Majesty. You are now queen of Aundria."

The doctor's words jerk me back. I force all my energy into turning to the group of lords walking steadily toward us, all their eyes on me. One by one they step forward, each bowing and kissing my hand.

My father is dead. And I am now queen.

———◄o►———

My face stings with tears. I hug my pillow, my stomach tense with crying. I don't know how long I lie there, drifting back and forth from the world like a fragile breeze.

My head drums like a thunderstorm as my gaze travels to the window. I lift myself from the pillow, my eyes blinking against the light. Wrapping my arms around myself, I wander over to stare out at the harbor. Yes, the Julinarin ship has pulled into port.

I lean my head against the glass as more tears inch down my cheeks. My breath forms a white circle on the window that soon melts back into nothing. I never knew loneliness feels so cold, like my very blood is slowly freezing to ice. All those I love are gone. Whether they're lying in a coffin or are halfway across the sea, they're not here anymore. I'm alone.

I will never leave thee nor forsake thee.

Jesus.

I've been ignoring Him, yet He is right beside me, reaching out His hand.

But the God who promised to be loving and faithful took my father. I press my fingers along the cold glass. How can I trust a God that allowed the death of a person I love so much?

I look up at the sky, my stomach sick. An icy chill seeps through the sill into my skin.

I turn away for the window, back to the empty room. Empty and dark. My eyes land on the Bible next to my bed. The fabric of my dress scratches my skin. After a moment, I walk over to it. My fingers slide over the cover as the book falls open:

There is a time for everything,
and a season for every activity under heaven:
a time to be born and a time to die,
a time to plant and a time to uproot,
a time to kill and a time to heal,
a time to tear down and a time to build,
a time to weep and a time to laugh,
a time to mourn and a time to dance,
a time to scatter stones and a time to gather them,
a time to embrace and a time to refrain,
a time to search and a time to give up,
a time to keep and a time to throw away,
a time to tear and a time to mend,
a time to be silent and a time to speak,
a time to love and a time to hate,
a time for war and a time for peace.

My breath catches in my throat. The fast beating of my heart calms as comfort and strength rush through my body. Quiet surrounds me, and I realize I'm on my knees.

He hasn't left me. He took my father home. And He holds me in His hands. How can I turn my back on a God that is so faithful to me even when I am not faithful to Him?

A knock sounds on the door. I look at the dark-brown wood. I can't stay in this room forever. Once the door opens, reality will return.

I cross to the mirror above my vanity. Red splotches shadow my eyes and darken the tip of my nose. Hair twists together across my head. Wrinkles dent my dress. I grasp a brush and drag it through my hair then straighten my dress and splash cold water on my face. I look at myself as the water drips off my chin and nose. My country needs me.

I walk to the door and pull it open. A servant and two knights stand before me. As they bow, the servant says, "Your Majesty, the duchess, Angelet of Julinar."

She steps to the side of the servants. I gasp and fly into her arms.

"Oh, Lorelle. Lorelle."

She holds me close, her hands pressing my back. I bury my head into her shoulder, disbelief and gratitude filling my heart.

Drawing away and grasping my hand, we walk into my bedchamber and close the door behind us. She wraps me into her embrace again. I press closer and close my eyes.

"I'm so sorry, Lorelle. I'm so sorry."

I eventually draw away from her and look her in the eye. "You have no idea how glad I am that you've come. I've been so lonely."

She clasps my hands. "My husband is in Alandar, and Lord Harmon is at the Julinarin estate. I came just to see you, but now, with the king's death, I know God had more of a reason for my coming." She squeezes my hands. "How are you feeling about everything?"

"I don't know!" I blurt out. "I don't know if I'm ready to be queen. And— my marriage."

"Yes, I heard of your marriage," she replies quietly.

I rub my face in my hands. "Angelet, I can't marry Prince Garreth."

She holds her arms at her middle. "Your feelings are perfectly normal. I felt the same way."

I stare at her. "Your marriage with Lord Barkinten was arranged?"

She gives a slow nod. "And oh, Lorelle, deep affection and trust for the other has formed between us."

"But love? Do you love him?"

"Yes, I do."

"But it's more of a forced love, isn't it?"

She lifts her chin. "I trust him, Lorelle. I depend on him. I have deep affection for him."

"A marriage needs more than affection," I say, crossing around the corner of the bed.

"A marriage needs trust," she answers. "And commitment. It needs patience … forgiveness." She smooths the edge of the cover on my bed. "He'll be different from you. You'll need to accept his differences. And he'll need to accept yours. You'll need to grow together." She looks up from the bed at me, her blue eyes bright. "And yes, I've grown to love Duke Barkinten with a real, genuine love. True, it did take some time and many hard, painful days, but now, nothing and no one is more important in my life than him."

I walk to the window again, trying to force my doubts away. Seconds pass before I eventually nod and say, "Thank you, Angelet. I'll remember what you said."

"Lorelle, stay strong. By the grace of God, you will get through this."

I move to the bed and sit down again, gathering part of the blanket in my hands.

She sets her hands in her lap. "If I tell you it will be easy and pleasant, I would be lying. But it does get easier after the first day. I promise. God is in control. You just need to let Him lead you into this marriage."

That's when I realize it. That's when I realize that no matter how much I worry and stress and try to prepare, what will happen will happen. God is in control, already holding my future and ready to lead me into it. I need to just trust Him that in the end, everything will be all right.

I shift my position. "How long will you be here?"

"Well, it depends on when the next Julinarin-bound ship leaves."

A small smile stretches my cheeks. "I can't tell you how glad I am that you've come."

She tilts her head, grinning back. "Your coronation will be held in two weeks, won't it?"

"Yes."

"Lord Williams told me everything. My, to see you sitting on that throne, saying your vows … I'll be so proud of you." She smooths a lock of hair from my forehead. "Whatever you feel like, I believe you are ready, Lorelle. I really do. A young woman of true integrity and noble character, who loves the Lord and is seeking after Him, you will carry Aundria very well. Very well indeed."

I lean back on my hands. "Why do you treat me like this?"

She cocks her head. "Like what?"

"You're always supporting me and caring for me. And you've never had to."

She brushes a hand over the back of her neck. "I've always wanted to. I love you like you're my own family." She pauses, a faint smile tinged by sadness curving her lips. "And I had a younger sister."

I frown, waiting for her next words.

"She died of typhoid fever when she was nine and I was eleven. It hurt me more than anything. We had been so close." She leans her arm on the bed, her dark lashes lowering over her eyes as she blinks. "You remind me of her."

I lean back in the study's chair, my neck warm beneath the sun's afternoon rays. "Then we know he will now need to live here, correct?"

"Correct, Your Majesty. I can request their presence in the conference room tomorrow at noon, if you wish."

I brush my hands over my skirt. "Thank you, Lord Conway. I would greatly appreciate it."

The lord turns and leaves Father's study. My study. Everything that was my father's is now mine—his rooms, lords, advisors, and his power and authority. I shake my head in disbelief.

Preparations for my coronation are being made faster than I can breathe. News that King Norman has passed away spread like fire all over the country. His death is changing everything, my upcoming marriage included. No one knew he would die so soon.

A knock sounds on my door. I bid the knocker enter, and a servant steps inside. "Your Majesty, the Alandarin ship has pulled into port."

Already? I'm surprised. The ship stood on the horizon early this morning, but I expected that it would lay anchor much later.

I thank the servant and leave the room. Lord Conway, two other lords, and a group of knights stride toward me.

"Your Majesty, if it is well with you, we shall go meet the Alandarin ship." Lord Conway extends his arm, his eyebrows raised in question. I nod and take his offer.

A small yet lavish carriage waits for us. After Lord Conway offers his hand and helps me in, I sink into the red plush seats and wait as the three other lords seat themselves. The knights mount the horses, and we lurch forward.

Black cloaks and black dresses cover the people of Kingston. When we ride into the village, instead of the usual cheering and waving hands, people nod their heads and bow out of reverence.

When we reach the harbor, memories splash over me at the sight of an Alandarin ship. In Alandar, I met two dear people who did so much for me, who saved my very life. So much happened to me in that country and because of that country.

A man with a green vest lined with gold meets us at the dock. Faint creases gather around his eyes, deepening when he smiles. "Greetings, Your Highness!" He kisses my hand and bows. "Allow me to introduce myself. I am Lord Henry Hemmings."

"I am honored to make your acquaintance, Lord Hemmings." Though we've never met, I remember him from years past as one of my father's most trusted lords from Julinar. It's no surprise he was sent to Alandar. "I am afraid you and the Alandarins have not yet heard of the sudden tragedy that has struck our nation. My father, King Norman, passed away one week ago."

Shock widens his eyes. "Oh, Your Majesty, I am so sorry. Truly, I am. He served our nation well and loyally. Please accept my deepest condolences."

"Thank you, Lord Hemmings," I whisper, a salty breeze wrapping around me. "His death is a tragic loss to us all. I will do everything in my power to carry on in his footsteps with dignity and strength."

A smile creases his cheeks. "I have no doubt you will." As he adjusts his vest, the lords with me cross the gangplank to discuss plans with two other lords on the ship. "When is your coronation?"

"In one week," I answer. A gull flaps its wings on the ship's mast. "Lord Hemmings, what news from Alandar?" I twist my fingers together.

"Alandar is reconstructing with great strength, integrity, and determination. The people there are growing out of their fright and are helping us. We have been rebuilding villages, reuniting families, and freeing slaves." The lord strokes his jaw. "Our leaders there are strong and determined. I have also brought some Alandarins with me. They wish to start a new life here or, as some of them were imprisoned, wish to continue the life they left behind."

I clasp my hands together. "Wonderful. I will be anxious to meet them." I smooth back a ringlet on my forehead. "Thank you, Lord Hemmings. It sounds like you are having success. When you return, I will send words of encouragement and support to them."

And maybe hear of Betsy and Martin.

———◄○►———

I hug my pillow and stare at the moon. Even though every inch of me aches with exhaustion, my mind refuses to sleep. Nestling deeper into the pillow, I break my bedroom's silence with a sigh that releases the tension cramping my shoulders.

I see my father's face, eyes twinkling and spilling over with love. I see my mother's smile lighting up the room and embracing me with security. I see Lord Wellington, running beside me, his sole mission to get me to safety on the night of the life-changing attack in Aundria. I see Betsy and Martin, spoon-feeding soup into my mouth with care so vivid I felt I could physically touch it. And I see James, looking at me with blue eyes filled with such passion and purpose my own eyes can't turn away.

Those people have changed my life. If there is ever a time that I want to thank them, that I want to tell them how much they mean to me, it is now.

—————◄◐►—————

My maid secures the diamond tiara in my wavy hair and then smiles at me in the mirror.

"Thank you, Felicity." I rise to my feet and walk to the door, ready to meet King Lionel and Queen Letha in the conference room.

I pull the knob and see Lord Hemmings walking up the stairs toward my room. As I step out, he extends his arm, and we walk down the staircase together.

When we reach the conference room, I walk through the doors. Late-morning sunlight streams through the huge windows on the room's other side. I cross to the table in the center, long and narrow like the room, and stand next to my chair.

Servants and soldiers take their positions against the wall. The sound of multiple footsteps nears the door. I place my hands at my sides and wiggle my shoulders.

The huge doors open, and a servant steps forward. "Their Majesties, King Lionel and Queen Letha of Lonegalde."

The king and queen enter, followed by a small selection of soldiers and servants. The three of us lower in formality according to the Aundrian custom, and then we all settle in our chairs at the table, the two of them across from me.

"Please accept our condolences concerning the death of your father." King Lionel looks at me from beneath bushy eyebrows.

I nod. "Thank you, Your Majesties."

King Lionel's eyebrows furrow together as he eyes me. His dark-brown hair lies ruffled beneath his crown, the same hair color as his wife's. Queen Letha's green, almond-shaped eyes stare at me with the same intensity as her husband's.

I fold my hands in my lap. "King Lionel, Queen Letha, thank you for coming to meet with me today. I am sure you must have an idea of why I asked for your presence today."

The faintest twitch of Queen Letha's eyebrow and lifting of King Lionel's chin tell me I am right.

"My father's death occurred at a much sooner time than any of us expected," I begin. "His death will alter many things, including the marriage between me and your son."

King Lionel cocks his head slightly to the side.

I set one of my hands on top of the other. "Now that I am queen, my duties dictate that I must remain here, in Aundria. Prince Garreth and I will have to live here instead of Lonegalde once we are married."

Queen Letha bends her neck, eyeing the wood table. King Lionel's eyes remain pinned on me. I keep my gaze on him.

For a moment, hope surfaces above my apprehension. If I have to marry someone I don't love, at least I can do it in an atmosphere I draw comfort from: my home.

The queen brings her gaze to her husband, and he looks back at her. She nods slightly.

They turn back to me. King Lionel says, "Queen Lorelle, my wife and I discussed this before we met with you. Prince Garreth's duty to his country cannot be fulfilled if he is to live here." He pauses and brings his hands together in his lap, his wife doing the same. "What we are saying, Your Majesty, is that we feel this marriage has now become unwise. With you ascending the throne and our son's duties calling him, we are not sure this marriage is the correct and wisest act."

I squeeze my fingers until they hurt, my stomach swimming. "Are Your Majesties suggesting we cancel the engagement?"

The king's eyes still on me, Queen Letha lifts her chin and says, "If we can do so peaceably and in agreement, yes."

I resist the urge to clap a hand to my chest in relief. "Your Majesties, I will consent to canceling this engagement."

The king tilts his chin. "Then we are in agreement and can part peaceably?"

I can't stop my smile. "We most certainly can."

The set lines in their faces ease as they nod. "It has been an honor to reside in your country again, Your Majesty," the queen says. "You would have made a fine wife for our son."

Yes, a fine wife, indeed.

The three of us rise, my heart pounding against my chest like a crashing wave.

"Thank you, Your Majesty." King Lionel's eyebrows move as he talks. "We will plan to depart in one week, if it is well with you."

Smiling at them, I nod. "My prayers will be with you."

They give me small smiles, and we all lower in formality, and then they leave the room, their footsteps echoing against the marble walls.

I swing to a servant by the wall. "Go and summon Angelet, please. Thank you."

As I wait for her to appear, I rush to the window, ignoring the soldiers' and servants' stares. Weights like rocks roll off my shoulders.

Oh, Jesus, thank You. Thank You!

He answered my prayer. Gratitude, excitement, and relief all well up inside me so much I think they will curl up and shoot out of me.

I turn to the window and look out, where the sea rolls its waves over each other. That same water carries a ship with a young man sailing on it—a young man who makes my heart leap just at the thought of him.

"Lorelle?"

I spin around to see Angelet standing in the doorway. As I clasp my hands together, I can hardly keep still. "Angelet, the meeting I just had with King Lionel and Queen Letha ... the engagement is off."

CHAPTER 23

I blink my eyes open. Sunlight shines ribbons of color through the glass of my window. Stretching my arms, I sit up. The blankets roll to the floor as I slide off the bed. Wrapping my arms around myself to fight off a chill, I walk to my balcony.

Outside, the clear morning air hugs me and whispers my senses awake. I close my eyes as the breeze plays with my hair. Nothing can compare to the sweet scent of a newly kissed morning, fresh from the maker's hands. I smile and open my eyes. Streaks of pink, red, orange, and yellow splash across the sky, clouds drifting past like painted fluffs. The Jasmin Sea swishes and splashes together, reflecting the sun's soft morning rays.

I curl my fingers over the cool marble of the railing. Today is my last day as a normal eighteen-year-old. I'm already queen, yes, but tomorrow the vows will be said, and a crown will be placed upon my head.

And I want to use every next day of my reign to glorify God.

Excitement races through me, competing with the doubts wriggling into my mind. I still can hardly grasp what I am about to become. Maybe it will take me years.

I scan the horizon, a perfect, sparkling line dipping into silver water. Somewhere, faraway, Alandar stands. Martin and Betsy are there now, undoubtedly rejoicing over what Alandar is becoming.

Bless them today, God.

I turn and slip back into my bedchamber then pull the braided cord that will summon my maids.

A sigh puffing my cheeks, I flop onto my bed, hugging a pillow. Tomorrow. Tomorrow.

But today ...

Reality strikes. Rising, I open my wardrobe doors and bring out a black satin gown, netted over with dark lace. I swallow. This is what I've selected to wear to my father's funeral.

The maids arrive to assist me. Cool satin slides down my body as they pull the gown over my shoulders. I stand still as their hands run over my skin, my eyes fixed on the sky past my window. The fabric pinches my breath away as they pin it at my back. With a final cinch they secure it and smooth down the ruffles.

I sit on the stool in front of my vanity, watching the mirror as their fingers lift and twist, intertwining and knotting my hair into a bun, allowing selected curls to tickle my neck.

My face disappears into a blur in the mirror. Never again will I bury my face in my father's velvet-covered chest or inhale his smell of wine. How I will miss laughing at his jokes and our deep conversations that seemed to last for hours.

"You are ready, Your Majesty."

The words jerk me back. I get up from the chair. A black bonnet has been placed on my head and a black, satin shawl over my shoulders. My maids' skirts fan out as they curtsy. Turning to the door, I open it and leave them behind.

Gray, milky light from the windowed walls fills the huge hall. I look through the glass, where I see thin, gray clouds blowing in. The trees and grass struggle to keep their original color under the sooty blanket.

Two waiting knights walk to me, one offering his arm. I break out of my stare and begin the descent down the staircase with them.

A pang of sorrow needles my stomach as I think of how God will truly be the only one beside me. Once Angelet returns to Julinar, I will be alone.

But I can't think about that now. Not now.

Lord Conway offers his arm as we reach the door. "Good afternoon, Your Majesty. Are you ready to depart?"

"I am, thank you." Outside, three other lords and eight soldiers join us. A tall golden carriage, intricately carved with flowers and roes, waits for us.

An icy wing stings my skin. Winter is coming.

After the four lords are seated in the carriage with me, the horses pull it from the palace yard. I bite my lip. I lean my head back against the cushioned wall and let the grayness of the sky swirl into my mind, drifting back to the past.

———◀◎▶———

"When are you going to blow that candle out?" I ask.

Father turns from the stack of papers on his desk and motions me in from the doorway, his face gentle and calm in the candlelight.

A soft chuckle leaves his lips. "Why are you still awake?"

I pull my robe tighter around my shoulders and pad to his desk. "I couldn't sleep. I went for a walk down the hall and saw light underneath your door."

He turns back to his tower of papers and rubs his forehead. "There's a lot of stress right now. The intensity of the war is beginning to take its effect on our people and forces." He blows his cheeks out with a sigh and pushes away his chair, allowing his legs to stretch out.

I lean my back against his desk and look at him. Soft silver strands peek through his hair. His brown eyes, bright and flecked with gold, shine in the candlelight.

"When will you be done?"

He grins at me. "Don't let me keep you up."

"You need your sleep." I straighten a pile of papers.

"My kingdom and my people come first. Once one has done everything one can do to uphold the protection of his or her people, then rest can come. That is when the work is truly fulfilling." He reaches up and fingers a loose curl at my throat. "You'll discover that one day, my love."

Gentle shadows from the candle swirl on the wall as he stands up, a smile of love and joy on his face. He takes my head in his hands and kisses my forehead. "You are your father's daughter. You are mine."

A blast of cold air strikes me as the carriage door swings open, bringing me back to the present. A footman stands at the steps, his gloved hand waiting for mine. I just want to get this over with, to have the church service already finished. I don't want to have to watch people take one last look at my father and pay their respects. I just want to be alone.

But this is for my father. I take the footman's hand and step out of the carriage.

The doors pull open, and we file into the church's cemetery. I breathe in through my nose and let out a quiet sigh through rounded lips.

One event is finished. I have only one more left.

I blink. The gray air has dissolved into a mist, where droplets of silver water hang almost visibly in midair. The wind pricks me, and my eyes sting. I don't know if it's from tears or the cold.

Lords and ladies form a mesh of black, with a few silver soldiers sprinkled throughout. As I cross over to them, my eyes travel above their faces to the tall, dark trees that stand like iron bars, locking in the cold. Blades of grass struggle to squeeze through hard dirt. Above me, a crow calls as it swoops through the air.

Anthony Chowtin, the tall, wiry minister, walks over to the sepulchre, its jewels glistening in the rain. My breath catches in my throat. The sepulchre holds generations of Aundrian royalty. My mother is among them.

And my father is about to join them.

A group of servants enter the graveyard carrying my father's coffin. I force my gaze away as we walk into the huge chamber and the people gather around.

The minister's voice drifts over my head. Every memory I have of my father rushes through my head. My mother's and his love were enough to sustain me on any day. Now that is all gone.

I pull my shawl tighter around my shoulders and swallow down a lump.

Then it's all over. He's buried and gone. A servant hands me a bouquet of flowers, and I gently place them on the tomb.

Then we are walking back to the carriage. I blink, sending more tears rolling down my cheeks. He is locked in that sepulchre and disappearing from me faster and faster by the second.

I creep into the carriage and sink against the cushions inside. My gaze shifts to the window, where the cold gray outside sifts into my bones.

We lurch and are on our way back to the palace. A soft tapping sounds on the carriage's roof. A misty breeze swirls inside. Rain.

Staring outside, a verse slides into my mind. "Even though I walk through the valley of the shadow of death, I will fear no evil, for you are with me; your rod and your staff, they comfort me."

———◄O►———

Moonlight takes command of the room as I blow out my candle then cross to my window. Raindrops slap the glass and slither down. I look at the moon, a steady beam of light in the dark clouds and thank my Savior for the gift of family—departed or present, blood-related or not, I thank Him.

I press my forehead against the cool glass, my thoughts flitting across the sea to James. My breath frosts into a white circle on the glass, and I shiver. What if he doesn't come back? Stories of sunken and attacked ships continuously crawl over the country.

What if something happens to his ship? I try to flick the thought away, straining my mind to focus on my coronation tomorrow.

But even that can't fully distract me from gazing at the sea where, somewhere, his ship sails.

CHAPTER 24

After throwing a cloak over my shoulders, I tie the strings into a bow beneath my chin and then turn for my door. Outside my room candlelight from the sconces bathes the air in a gold glow, so warm and smooth I feel I can almost touch it. I start toward the staircase when I hear a door open and shut. Angelet crosses to me.

"Why, Lorelle, wherever are you going?"

I pull the cloak further around my shoulders. "I'm taking a walk outside the palace."

"It's already dark."

"I've been waiting for the weather to clear. I won't be gone long. I just want to collect my thoughts before tomorrow—and tonight." At the moment, the idea of speaking with groups and groups of lords and ladies at the traditional night-before-coronation reception only brings me stress.

She nods. "I understand. Enjoy it, my dear."

Smiling, I lean forward and kiss her cheek. I then slip past her and hurry down the stairs. Four soldiers stand waiting at the door.

"Thank you, men. I am ready."

"Shall we bring a lantern, Your Majesty?"

I shake my head. "No, thank you. I will be fine without it."

The doors open, revealing the starry, sapphire-blue night. I half-walk-half-run down the entrance stairs, excitement to be outside on such a beautiful night bubbling inside me. The lights of Kingston glitter like candles, and a gentle, sweet breeze swirls through the air.

Stopping, I close my eyes. I love being surrounded by the pure moonlight. I breathe in. These are the last few hours before the event that will change my life.

Opening my eyes, I swing toward the gate. The sound of the leaves rustling in the trees and the waves lapping onto the shore soothes me like a whisper. My thoughts drift to my father. Yes, he is all right. He has gone home.

Behind me, the four soldiers keep a steady distance. I continue strolling past the village. I'm nearing the harbor, where the Aundrian ships appear as black shadows drifting on the water— except for one. The waves separate as it steers into port.

The four soldiers are instantly beside me. The ship pulls into the docks, and by the moon's light I see sailors rushing around on the ship's main deck. The gangplank is placed, and two tall, dark figures filter through the sailors and stride across it. When their heads turn our direction, they step into the moonlight. I gasp.

"Captain Carrington of the *Tanner*," Captain Carrington announces, his low voice rumbling into my ears.

"Ja— Sir Wellington! Captain Carrington!" I exclaim. "How was your voyage?"

They walk to us and rise from a bow. "More successful than we could have hoped," the captain answers. "We have brought back large amounts of Gadelin's rich fruit."

"I am pleased." I stop myself from stealing a glance at James.

The captain's eyes shine. "Yes, we were very lucky."

As he continues telling us more of his success, my eyes succeed in escaping to James. A guarded smile lights his face. I suck in a breath.

"… and we are now glad to be home," the captain finishes. He tips his hat. "It was a pleasure seeing you again, Your Highness, but if you will excuse me, I must see to my cargo."

I nod. "Certainly, Captain. A pleasure seeing you again."

After a bow, he turns and heads for the gangplank.

James's blue eyes remain pinned to mine as the captain walks away. Hesitation etches over his features. We both open our mouths to speak when the Captain calls from the gangplank, "Wellington!"

He rubs a hand over his mouth. I shift my position, and after a quick bow he turns and hurries back to the ship.

Standing for a minute, I stare at his dark figure rushing across the main deck, my heart pounding in my chest. He's returned safely.

"Shall we move onward, Your Majesty?" a soldier asks.

I watch the activity on the ship, singling out one figure. The moonlight throws soft shadows over the deck, broken up by patches of silver light.

"Your Majesty?"

I almost jump.

The soldier motions onward.

I turn away and continue walking, the ship's commotion behind me.

—◄◯►—

"Then Captain Carrington and any lords and knights on board will be able to attend the reception?"

"I assume so," I answer, shifting my position in front of my vanity and loosening a pin one of my maids has just pushed into my hair.

Angelet's eyes search mine. "I hope you will enjoy your night then."

I turn back to the mirror.

She touches a hand to my cheek. "You're still warm after your walk."

I grin, looking out at the moonlight through my window. The leaves of a tree next to my window ruffle in the night breeze. I was out in that beautiful night just minutes ago.

"You are finished, Your Majesty." One of the maids secures the last pin in my hair.

"Thank you, ladies." As I stand, they curtsy and file out of the bedchamber.

The fabric tickles my fingers as I smooth my dress. "I could have stayed outside all night." I blow out air. "I'm nervous."

She leans her head against the wall. "I know. I will be there with you and so will Lord Harmon."

I nod. I was so relieved when the lord returned from his trip two days earlier. Already I feel safer.

She walks to me and twirls one of my curls around her finger. "You are a daughter of the king, whether he is the one who is only with you in spirit or the One who died for you." She kisses the top of my head. "Remember that."

I clasp her hand and lean my forehead against hers. "Thank you."

I bite my lip. I miss him so much. I'm about to take his place as ruler, and that sweeps a bittersweet feeling over me that I can't really explain.

Angelet squeezes my hand as a knock sounds on the door. She turns and pulls it open. Lord Harmon stands in the doorway.

I look up at him, nerves stiffening my brow. The corners of his eyes wrinkle as he gently smiles. He holds out a hand to me. I grasp it and find myself letting him draw me into a hug. I relax my head on his chest and close my eyes. Funny, how his vest smells just like my father's.

We descend the staircase and cross to the room where the reception is being held. The doors open when we reach them, revealing the large room filled with lords, ladies, dukes, and duchesses. I catch myself before I begin looking for my father, waiting for him to give me a nod or message with his eyes.

Lord Harmon's arm slips beneath mine, and I see Angelet beside me. Together, we walk to the front of the room where I mount the dais. As the crowd quiets, I look over the room. Captain Carrington stands near the hall. It only takes two more seconds to find James's blue eyes and blond hair. Silence pounds in my ears as his gaze meets mine.

Finally, I open my mouth to speak. "Fellow friends and countrymen, I am honored to be standing here before you today. My father left behind him a rich legacy. He built ahead of him a path of honor and purpose for me to follow. I will do everything within my power and ability to serve and lead Aundria with the dignity and strength my father carried."

The crowd erupts into applause, and knights pound their feet. I squeeze the sides of my skirt, smiling. "The pride I have in my country is indescribable. We have endured contempt, pushed through opposition, and persevered through trial without wavering. We are loyal, dedicated, and faithful, standing firm through any storm as one nation." I scan the room, catching the gazes of the smiling people, their eyes bright with hope. "I see now that our country has been blessed by an almighty and all-powerful God. He has protected and strengthened us, and it is by His Hand that we are the country we are today."

I see all eyes are fixed on me, everyone waiting for my next words. "A number of you are aware of what I am going to say next. My engagement with Prince Garreth of Lonegalde has been canceled. He and King Lionel and Queen Letha have returned to their home country." I steal a look at James. Disbelief widens his eyes.

The rest of the time passes in a blur. I go through the motions of the formal greetings and discussing the coronation and Aundria's laws. By the end, I am ready to retreat to my room. Excitement mixed with nerves makes me anxious to get some space to think. My heart has been racing all night.

---◄O►---

I can't sleep. I roll over and stare at the ceiling, my hand hot on my hot forehead. Untangling my feet from the covers, I pull myself off the bed. Grabbing my robe, I slide into my slippers and open a small drawer in my desk. My fingers wrap around the key at the back of it, and after shutting it, I cross to the door. Slowly opening it, I slip out.

The light from the sconces have been replaced by darkness, but by the moonlight streaming in from the castle's large windows, I can see guards posted here and there throughout the hallways.

Pulling my robe tighter around myself, I move to the stairs and quickly walk down. I hear a door open and close but ignore it and hurry down a hallway hidden in the dark until I come to the door I am looking for, a quiet one tucked away in the west side of the castle. I used it to sneak out many times when I was younger.

Looking around and seeing no one, I take the key and slide it into the lock, turning it until I hear a soft click. Then, I pull it open and step out, shutting it behind me.

The moonlight swirls through the sweet air, so cool on my body. The garden I enter is exactly as I left it. The same tree crouches by the door. I've nestled under its branches so many times in the past.

I walk out farther into the moonlight. Somehow the day has worn me emotionally. Maybe it was reliving all the memories of my family. I swallow a lump in my throat as my eyes become hot with tears. I miss my father more than any human should be allowed to miss someone.

Blinking them away, I look up to the stars and think of the hands that made them. I feel God's love sweep through me, so gentle but so powerful.

Footsteps clicking in the hallway on the other side of the door shatter the silence. I swallow. If I am found out here alone, without a chaperone, at night ...

The doorknob turns, and James steps out.

I stare at him. "What ... what are you doing here?"

He shuts the door behind him then turns to me. "I saw you come down."

I lower my head, my neck warm.

He eases closer to me. "I am so, so sorry about your father. I wish there was something I could say, but ..." He stops. "Our nation will miss a strong and noble king."

I give him a small smile. "He's gone home."

After a second, he reaches out to touch my cheek. "May I ... may I take you for a moonlit ride?"

I almost laugh. "A moonlit ride?" A smile tugs at the corners of my mouth. "Perhaps. What would be our mode of transportation, may I ask?"

"Horses."

"Ah, horses." I pause for a moment, excitement speeding up my heartbeat. "Well, I accept."

A grin spreads across his face. "Let me fetch two horses from the stable. Would you mind waiting?"

"Not at all."

For a second, he merely looks at me, and then he turns and opens the door and is gone.

My breathing is the only thing I can hear in the night, minus the occasional whisper of the wind through the leaves. I sit down against the tree and curl up my knees, wrapping my arms around them and feeling my heart beat against my chest.

The sound of horses cantering finally cuts through the still night. I look up. Two horses circle the castle, one with a rider.

He slows them to a stop and then slides to the ground. Walking over to me, he stretches his hand out toward mine.

I grin and clasp it, letting him pull me up. He leads me to a chestnut-colored gelding with a white stripe down his nose. Gripping my waist, he lifts me up. Once I'm situated, he mounts his own and then casts a grin at me. "Ready?"

I smile. "Ready."

We take off at a canter. The wind rifles through my hair, pulling it loose from my braid until it flies free. I turn my head to the man riding next to me. He sits tall and erect in the saddle, a smile refusing to leave his face.

A smile won't leave mine, either. We ride through a pasture, the grass glistening with dew, and then enter a thin, small wood with a clear path in the middle. Moonlight filters through the treetops, reflecting off the leaves and laying gentle, silver fingers on us, just enough light to break the soft dark. This night is perfect. Though we say nothing, it's enough. It's enough.

Once we leave the wood, we come to a small clearing next to a quiet, secluded beach. Easing the horses to a trot, we head for the sand. The sea sparkles like jewels, the moon shining above. The waves, splashing and rolling onto the shore, sound like a sweat melody, the rustling leaves whispering in the trees.

When we reach the beach, James dismounts and crosses to me. He reaches up and lifts me off the horse. Once my feet hit the ground, we stop, standing in each other's arms.

After a moment, he clasps my hand and leads me to the water. Both of us silent, we settle onto the soft sand, the water glistening and splashing just at the tips of our feet.

He leans closer to me and gently puts his arm around my shoulders. "Lorelle," he says, "there's something I've been wanting to tell you for a long time. Just as I was getting the nerve to, you told me you were engaged."

I breathe in, waiting for his next words. After a pause, he finally speaks. "I ... love you, Lorelle."

My heart leaps. "I love you too, James."

He moves closer to me, his fingers twining with mine. "Even from the moment we met, I knew you were beautiful, inside and out. I saw your passion, your courage, your caring spirit. And your heart ... it has changed into something even more beautiful." He pauses. "You have captivated me."

I can practically feel my heart filling up to the brim, ready to overflow. A salty breeze rustles over us and ripples his white shirt.

His fingers tighten around mine. "I want to protect you, Lorelle. I want to give you joy. I want to be there for you, every single moment of every day. I want to comfort you, to encourage you, to care for you, to love you."

"James, I—" I stop, staring into his eyes, the blue eyes I've wondered at for so long. They belong to the man who has risked his life for me—who loves me.

"I never want you to be alone," he says.

I release a breath of pure, overwhelming joy. His eyes are inches from mine. Deep down, I feel God overflowing my heart because He looks down at me, little me, and sees me as His daughter who needs love. And now His love is simply and beautifully abounding.

"I would give my life for you," he continues. "Again and again I would give my life for you, because I love you."

My heart soars. He moves closer to me, his arms around me, his blue eyes holding mine. When he speaks next, he robs me of breath.

"Will you marry me, Lorelle?"

I bring my hand to his face, watching the breeze ruffle his blond hair. My heart whirls with excitement and joy. Looking into his blue eyes, I whisper, "Yes, I'll marry you, James. I'll marry you."

In the quiet of the night, with the waves lapping onto the shore beside us, he leans in and brings his lips to mine. I close my eyes and let him draw me closer, wrapped in his embrace. The love that sweeps over me threatens to soar out into the night and up to the stars, so strong and powerful but so gentle and tender. This is love. And I know that we can love because He first loved us.

CPSIA information can be obtained at www.ICGtesting.com
Printed in the USA
LVOW12s2041020215

425368LV00003B/8/P

9 781490 847474